KU-682-653

She-Clown

and Other Stories

Hannah Vincent

myriad

First published in 2020 by
Myriad Editions
www.myriadeditions.com

Myriad Editions
An imprint of New Internationalist Publications
The Old Music Hall, 106–108 Cowley Rd, Oxford OX4 1JE

First printing
1 3 5 7 9 10 8 6 4 2

Copyright © Hannah Vincent 2020
The moral right of the author has been asserted

All rights reserved. No part of this publication may be
reproduced, stored in a retrieval system, or transmitted in
any form or by any means without the written permission
of the publisher, nor be otherwise circulated in any form of
binding or cover other than that in which it is published and
without a similar condition being imposed on the
subsequent purchaser

A CIP catalogue record for this book
is available from the British Library

ISBN (pbk): 978-1-912408-38-2
ISBN (ebk): 978-1-912408-39-9

Designed and typeset in Palatino
by WatchWord Editorial Services, London

Printed and bound in Great Britain
by Clays Ltd, Elcograf S.p.A.

Praise for *She-Clown and Other Stories*

'Hannah Vincent practises a sort of believe-it-or-not deadpan surrealism to write about what really interests her—people, humanity, how we all get on, or get along or, in some cases, just get by. *She-Clown* is an excellent example.'
—Nicholas Royle, editor of *Best British Short Stories*

'Hannah Vincent's short stories are fictional sisters of Judy Chicago's epic feminist artwork *The Dinner Party*. The language, the worlds and the characters are glorious.'   —Julia Crouch

'Hannah Vincent's stories are as minimal as Raymond Carver, and as clever as Raymond Carver: nothing is ever as it seems then you turn the page and are surprised again.' —Lisa Blower

'Hannah Vincent writes tight, spares no words and pulls no punches. From clown paint to oesophageal frogs, her stories are often strange, always sharp and like to linger.'   —Alice Slater

Praise for Hannah Vincent's novels

Alarm Girl

'A book of heat, loss, wit and aching tenderness.'
—Tim Crouch

'Beautifully written; the heat and landscapes of South Africa leap off the page as Indy's story unfolds.'   *—Bella*

'An assured exposition of grief, belonging and the nature of self. Conv   of South Africa an   e into a book whi   *ex Life*

9030 00007 0893 5

'Sensitively written, this is a heartrending tale of a young girl trying to make sense of her life while accepting loss and change.'

—We Love This Book

'In tone and content I could compare it to Nathan Filer's *The Shock of the Fall*... A subtle and yet powerful novel...'

—Writers Hub

'Beautiful, moving and achingly human.'   —Spirit FM

'A hugely sating read. Compelling, beautiful and poetic, this is a book to get utterly lost in.'

—Bookgroup.info

The Weaning

'An original, surprising, beautifully crafted novel that stands out from the crowd ... packs a powerful punch ... pared down ... enthralling ... a great achievement.'   —Anya Lipska

'A gripping page-turner.'   —Paul McVeigh

'Blown away by this book...without doubt a full-on five-star read.'   —Bookish Chat

'A beautifully written, evocative and very dark story that explores issues that will resonate with the reader. Hannah Vincent is a talented observer; she sees life and people and relates them through her books with incredible insight. Fluent and powerful, I loved this book, just as I adored her first!'

—Random Things Through My Letterbox

To Mum and Dad

LONDON BOROUGH OF WANDSWORTH	
9030 00007 0893 5	
Askews & Holts	
AF	
	WW19018690

Contents

Portrait of the Artist

CARINA'S MOTHER stared at the man's penis. It was misshapen, like a dahlia tuber, with pendulous balls hanging below. The name 'Leonardo' was written in different coloured letters in an arc above the drawing, like a rainbow. The classroom clock ticked softly. She heard her husband's stomach rumble. A casserole she had made was waiting for them at home.

The classroom door banged.

'Sorry to keep you,' the teacher said, breezing in.

She was young, with neat, fine hair and interesting clothes. She pulled out a chair on the other side of the desk, and thanked Carina's parents for coming. Carina's mother glanced at the picture on the wall again. The life-sized figure was contained inside a pencilled square, which was surrounded by a circle. There were two pairs of arms and two pairs of legs. She stared at the carefully drawn penis and wondered if it was this young teacher who had drawn the man so lovingly.

Carina was a lively member of the class, the teacher said, with successful friendships and an interest in history. She would be a candidate for one of the good universities, if that was what they wanted for her? And what Carina wanted, of course.

'University's what we want for her, yes,' Carina's father told the teacher, and Carina's mother nodded in agreement, conjuring a mental picture of their daughter in a graduation gown, a scroll balanced lightly in her hands. She hoped Carina would find the casserole when she got back from her netball match. She had left her a note.

'Good,' the teacher said, smiling.

She wore coral lipstick and round glasses with tortoiseshell frames. Maybe Carina would be a teacher one day.

'Now then, the reason I called you in today was this,' the teacher said, opening a drawer in her desk and pulling out a sheaf of papers. She handed Carina's father a few sheets from the top of the pile. He reached for his reading glasses, inside the briefcase by his feet. Watching him, Carina's mother spotted a button lying on the classroom carpet and bent forward to pick it up. It was black, probably off a school skirt, or a schoolboy's trousers.

The teacher gave Carina's mother some pages, too, but Carina's mother didn't have to read them to know what was written there. She lay them on her lap and pressed the button into the palm of her hand, felt its indentation. Scanning the paper, she recognised her daughter's distinctive handwriting—her fancy As and exuberant Ys—and she experienced the same light-headedness she felt when she discovered the pages underneath Carina's bed.

She had been hunting for last summer's plimsolls to take to the shoe bank—Carina had a new pair of trainers. She was growing fast. She was a young woman now. She had started her periods while they were on holiday. Several packs of sanitary pads with French writing on, which they had bought from the campsite supermarket, were stashed under the bed, alongside a violin case, some old board games and puzzles, and this sheaf of papers. Carina's mother had assumed the pages were homework, and she sat back on her heels to see if she could understand any of it. It was a test she set herself, fully expecting not to comprehend what her daughter had written, but expecting also to find this lack of understanding a pleasure.

The violence of the first few sentences made her catch her breath. She glanced quickly around the room, as if someone was watching her. Then she shoved the papers away from her and staggered to her feet, her heart beating fast, her breath coming in short, painful gasps. She nudged the pile of paper with the toe of her slipper, as if it was a dead thing. Then, trying not to read what her daughter had written, she crouched down, shuffled the pages into a neat stack, and quickly stuffed them back where she had found them.

For the rest of the afternoon she polished and tidied Carina's room, dusting with a cleaning rag made from a pair of her husband's old pyjamas, soft from years of washing. She rearranged the furniture, dragging the bed out from behind the door, vacuuming underneath it and heaving it to a new position underneath the window, taking care to replace the sheaf of papers along with the jigsaw puzzles and the violin in its case. When Carina came home from school, she approved of the changes her mother had made, saying how much easier it would be to concentrate at her desk now it wasn't facing the window.

Later that same night, after her husband had gone to bed, Carina's mother crept into her daughter's room, like she used to on Christmas Eve. Instead of leaving presents, she took the sheaf of papers from under the bed and read them in the bathroom with the door locked.

Afterwards, with her husband and daughter still sleeping, she went downstairs to the kitchen and made herself a drink. Sipping the hot chocolate, she went through the collection of old clothes she kept for cleaning rags, cutting up a nightie of Carina's and a faded T-shirt of her own with the kitchen scissors. She snipped off the yellowed front section of some of her husband's underwear, and then, with a needle and thread taken from the sewing box she inherited from her own mother, she began to stitch the pieces together. At other times, the neighbourhood was full of noise—of strimmers and lawn-mowers and next door's radio—but there, in the kitchen, in the middle of the night, everything was quiet. The weather was so mild, she opened the back door. A fox came sniffing right up to the house, stared her in the eye, then ran away.

Now, her husband was reading the words that had caused her those sleepless nights. She concentrated on the steady tick of the classroom clock, and on the feel of the found button between her finger and thumb. Next to the drawing of the naked man was a list of facts about Leonardo da Vinci's life. Leonardo was a genius. Leonardo was a vegetarian. Leonardo's mother was a peasant girl. The colouring in of the letters that spelled his name was extremely neat, with a red *L*, yellow for the *E*, pink for the *O*, a green *N*. There was no repetition, except for the final *O* which was pink, the same as the first one. At last, her husband looked up.

'I can see why you wanted to show us this material,' he said, removing his reading glasses.

'It's strong stuff, isn't it?' the teacher said.

'Strong's one word for it,' he said. 'Is it normal for a young girl to write this kind of thing?'

'My question is, why does she *want* to write about these things?' the teacher said, leaning forward and looking at them both, her eyes magnified behind her glasses.

Carina's mother looked away, her gaze dragged back to the naked man. Faintly sketched lines suggested pubic hair.

'It's the world we live in, isn't it?' she said, forcing herself to look at her husband and the young teacher.

'Well, I don't know what world you live in!' her husband said.

His face was flushed, and she could see a small patch of bristles in the hollow of his throat where he had missed a bit when shaving.

'Have you discussed Carina's writing with her?' the teacher asked.

'We had no idea she was writing,' Carina's father said. He turned to his wife. 'Did we?'

The fingers of the man in the drawing were touching the outer edges of the square. His naked feet were resting on the tangent point where circle met square.

'Did we?' her husband asked her once more.

Was the circle inside the square, or was it the other way around?

'I suggest you take this home and have a chat with her,' the teacher said, holding out the sheaf of papers to Carina's father. He took the pages and thrust them inside his briefcase.

'Give me a call if you or Carina would like me to make an appointment with the school counsellor,' the teacher said.

They made their way through the empty school corridors to the car park and drove home through rainy streets without speaking.

Indoors, Carina was waiting for them, sitting on the bottom stair with wet hair. She was already in her nightie. Her slippers had puppy faces and floppy ears on each toe.

'What did she say?'

'She wanted to talk about your writing,' Carina's father said, meeting his daughter's gaze. He brought the bundle of papers out of his briefcase.

Carina scowled, spots of pink appearing on her face and neck.

'She's worried, Cari,' her father said. 'We all are.'

'Worried about what?' Their daughter's eyes brimmed.

'Worried about you—about why you would write such things.'

Carina snatched the papers and scrambled up the stairs, clutching her writing, stumbling as she went. Her mother gathered the damp netball kit that lay on the hallway floor. She would carry it to the washing machine on her journey to heat up the casserole, imagining, as she always did, a thread extending from her body, creating an intricate web as she weaved in and out of rooms on her daily business, tidying and dusting and polishing. Picking up the netball kit meant that loading the washing machine and preparing dinner could be contained within one movement—if she left it there, to see to later, there would be a messy tangle of thread. She tried not to double back on herself, in order to maintain a clean line.

'You wrote those things down—are you saying you didn't want anyone to read them?' her husband called after their daughter.

A door slammed as Carina's mother moved towards the kitchen. She heard her husband tread carefully up the stairs, heard him tap on Carina's bedroom door, heard their daughter tell him to go away.

'I'm coming in, Carina. I'd like to talk to you.'

The casserole she had cooked remained untouched. The round dish stood neatly in the middle of a square, woven placemat. The note she had written lay next to it. She loaded the netball kit into the washing machine, glancing at her daughter's name written on the inside of her sports shirt collar in fabric pen. One day it would be written on the door to a classroom, or an executive office, or on the front of a history text book, or on a foundation stone, even.

She scooped washing powder from a box in the kitchen cupboard. Reaching behind the box, she fetched out a small, cloth doll. She had drawn its eyes and nose and mouth in fabric pen. She stroked its hair, made from the frayed laces of outgrown plimsolls, and held the dolly briefly against her cheek. Then she slipped a hand into her pocket and took out the button she had found in the classroom. She held it against one of the dolly's drawn-on eyes and was pleased with the effect. It brought her to life. She hid the doll among the polishes and detergents once more, along with the button. She would sew it on tonight, when the rest of the world was asleep.

Fireflies

CAZ WAS IN the kitchen making sandwiches with the woman. The man was doing the washing up, standing at the sink with his back to them, a tea towel draped over one shoulder. The tea towel had pictures of churches printed on it. The woman sawed at a loaf of bread sitting on the breadboard. The loaf was round and the breadboard was round too. Caz unwrapped her own loaf from its plastic bag and spread two slices with salad cream then sprinkled on cheese the woman had grated. She cut the sandwich into quarters, then cut each quarter in half again so there were eight small fingers. She laid them on a plate the woman handed her, brushing off seeds from the woman's bread that had stuck to it. They waited for the kettle to boil.

The couple made them sit at the table every mealtime.

'We think it's important to eat together as a family,' the woman said.

'We aren't family,' Caz said.

Social services had arranged for her and Jude to be temporarily re-housed after what her key worker referred to as 'the incident'. Luke wasn't allowed to know where she was, and Caz wasn't even sure herself. It had taken a long car journey to get here.

They carried their drinks and sandwiches into the room the man and woman called 'the conservatory', where Jude was waiting for them.

'How comes you got a highchair?' Caz asked. 'You got grandkids?'

'We tend to foster quite a few babies,' the woman said.

Caz handed Jude a piece of sandwich. Jude watched the man walk around the table. The man pulled out a chair and sat down. He took the tea towel off his shoulder and folded it into a neat square, smoothing it out with both hands on the table in front of him.

'We've got some news,' the woman said.

'Yeah?' Caz said.

The woman and the man looked at each other. Caz moved the piece of sandwich closer to Jude's mouth, but he wasn't paying attention, he was looking at the man.

'It might be a little difficult,' the woman said. 'You need to prepare yourself.'

The conservatory roof was one massive skylight. At night you could see stars, but in daytime it was so bright it gave Caz a headache.

'Spit it out,' she said.

'Luke's social worker has been in touch and they want to arrange contact.'

'Fuck that.'

The man kept smoothing the square of his tea towel.

'Obviously any visit would be supervised.'

'He's not getting contact.'

'I know it's hard—'

'He's not fucking getting it!'

They didn't understand. Luke didn't want to see Jude—he was doing it to wind her up. His name on her arm was one thing, she could always get laser removal, but like a twat she had it written on Jude's birth certificate. She gave up on the sandwich and lifted Jude's beaker to his lips, nudging it against his mouth to make him drink. The bruising around his eye had faded from purple to yellow, it would be gone soon.

On the day of 'the incident', she had taken Jude into town. It was raining and the plastic cover on his buggy didn't fit properly. She ducked inside a supermarket where a security guard followed her down one of the aisles.

'I'm not on the rob, if that's what you think,' she told him, slipping a tube of foundation up her sleeve.

'No, you're waiting for the rain to stop.'

'Thass right.'

'It's stopped.'

She flicked a finger at him and left. The hems of her track-suit slapped on the wet pavements all the way home.

Her key worker was always telling her how lucky she was to have her flat, but her key worker didn't have to drag Jude's buggy up six sets of stairs every time she came home. She paused for breath on the second landing. They were always on at her to give up smoking.

There was a shuffling behind her neighbour's door and she could hear the chain being drawn across from the inside.

She waited for the girl to emerge.

'Alright?' Caz said.

The girl gave a kind of smile.

'Pissing down,' Caz told her.

She watched as the girl manoeuvred her pram out on to the landing.

'Mind them stairs, they're slippery as fuck.'

The girl nodded. She waited while Caz moved past her.

'Getting big,' Caz said, glancing inside the girl's pram. 'Jude'll have to watch out for him—reckon he could have him, easy!'

She was sweating by the time she reached the door of her flat. The bass from Luke's music vibrated through her fingers as she slotted her key into the lock. When she stepped inside, the air was heavy with weed.

Luke was sitting on the sofa. He had his boots on and he was wearing proper trousers instead of trackies. She parked the buggy and crossed the room to push a window open as far as it would go, which wasn't far because of the catch. They were scared people would top themselves.

'What the fuck are you doing?'

'Opening a window for his asthma, you retard.' She turned the music down. 'Got you something.' She fetched the tube of make-up from the bottom of the buggy and chucked it at him. It landed in his lap.

'What's this shit?' He turned the make-up over in his hands, pretending to read the packaging. 'I ain't wearing make-up.'

'There's no point getting done up like a twat and going in with a black eye,' Caz said.

'Who are you calling a twat?'

She peeled off her wet jacket and top and sat on his lap, facing him in just her bra, her legs straddled wide.

'Steady,' Luke said, placing his hands on her hips.

Her hair was wet from the rain. She squeezed the moisture from her ponytail and water ran in thin rivulets between her breasts.

'Getting me wet,' he said, pushing her off him.

She went into the bathroom to get a towel. She rubbed her hair dry and checked her reflection in the mirror. When she came back into the living room, Luke had his eyes closed and his head was resting against the back of the sofa. One of his eyelids was dark purple. Jude murmured in his buggy. Caz took him out and put him on the floor. He crawled over to the Xbox.

'Jude, no.' She picked him up again and sat him on Luke's lap.

'Hello, little man,' Luke said, opening his eyes.

She sat next to them on the sofa and unscrewed the cap on the tube of foundation. She squeezed a blob of cream on to her finger. Jude watched.

'Come here,' she said, shuffling closer.

He looked handsome in his interview clothes. The diamond stud in his ear glittered in the smoky room, reminding her of the tiny dots of light she had seen in Corfu on the walk back from the bar at night. The guy her mum was dating said they were fireflies. She went to dab foundation around Luke's eye, but he jerked his head away.

'D'you think I'm a faggot?'

'You said it, not me,' she said, laughing, and she reached out towards him again, with the make-up on her finger.

The force of the blow knocked the tube out of her hand and sent it flying. She heard her jaw crack and felt Jude's body tumble against hers as he fell off the sofa. Everything went dark, then pinpricks of light danced in front of her eyes.

. . .

Now, Jude had a black eye to match his father's. The bruise had faded from purple to yellow since they'd been living with the couple. It would be gone soon.

Her key worker asked her how she planned to turn her life around now that Luke was off the scene. Trouble was, he wasn't off the scene, was he? She had wiped his number off her phone, but he was Jude's dad, and now his social worker was arranging for him to have contact.

The night before the contact meeting she couldn't sleep. She snuck downstairs in her pyjamas and smoked a cig outside the back door. There were so many stars she knew she must be a long way from a town. The car journey to get here had taken hours, and tomorrow they would make the same journey back again and Luke would get to hold Jude and play with him while she was somewhere else. She wondered if he was awake, and if he was, whether he was thinking about her.

'Can't sleep?' The woman came to stand next to her on the back step.

Caz breathed out a plume of smoke and they both watched it drift upwards in the dark night air.

The woman pulled the back door quietly shut behind her and shivered. She was wearing a cardigan over her nightie.

'It's supervised contact only, Caz. His social worker will be there the whole time. Jude will be perfectly safe.'

The woman wrapped her cardigan more tightly around herself. 'We could go to the shops or a café afterwards. Do something nice,' she said.

Caz stubbed out her cigarette in a saucer she kept on the kitchen windowsill.

'The important thing is to keep a cool head,' the woman said. 'It's not ideal and it's not what you want, but—'

'He's Jude's dad. He's got a right to see him,' Caz said, pressing the dead cigarette into the flower pattern in the middle of the saucer.

'You're being very mature about this. I can't tell you how impressed I am with your attitude.'

Caz took a deep breath.

'That's right, remember your breathing exercises.'

The woman suggested they turn in now, as tomorrow would be a long day.

The next day, Caz got up early, before Jude was even awake, and put on her white top and her big hoop earrings. Outside the house it was dark, but she could hear the man and the woman moving around downstairs. She scraped her hair into a high ponytail, watching herself in the mirror as she fastened it with a hair elastic.

The man helped her strap Jude into his car seat, then he got into the driving seat. The woman sat next to her husband in the front of the car, while Caz sat next to Jude in the back.

'All set?' the man asked, and the woman turned around to face Caz and asked if she had everything she needed.

The man started the engine. It had been night-time when they made this journey before. After the fight with Luke, Caz could barely remember the drive. She had seen motorway signs flashing past, and the red tail lights of other cars, but that was all. Now, in daylight, she looked out of the window at fields of cows and sheep. One field had a burnt-out tree in the middle and the man told a story about a herd of cows who were electrocuted when their drinking trough was struck by lightning.

They stopped at motorway services for the man to stretch his legs. The woman brought out a bag of sandwiches she had made for the journey and they ate them at a wooden picnic table perched on a grassy bank. There was a play area where children in coats and mini puffer jackets slid down a slide and dangled from a small climbing frame. Caz sat Jude on her lap. She picked the seeds out of the bread and tore the crusts off the woman's sandwiches.

'Do you think we should change him?' the woman asked.

They went to the toilets and the woman jangled her keys in Jude's face while Caz cleaned his bum.

'More than he deserves,' Caz said as they walked back to the car. 'Should have given him Jude with a shitty arse.'

It was beginning to spot with rain. They hurried back to the car and strapped themselves back in.

'All set?' the man said.

Fields and farms began to give way to furniture warehouses as they drew closer to the town. The rain grew heavier and the man increased the speed of the windscreen wipers. At a crossing where the railway met the road, they had to wait in a queue of traffic for a train to go past. The man switched off the car engine and drummed his fingers on the steering wheel.

'Look, Jude—choo-choo train!' the woman said, turning around in her seat to look at him, but Jude was watching the man's hands on the steering wheel and the train whooshed by so fast he missed it.

When the man started up the engine once more, the woman started up about doing something nice.

'We could take Jude to the library afterwards,' she said. 'He might like it there.'

'You sound like my key worker,' Caz said. 'She's always on about the library.'

'It's not just books,' the woman said. 'They have games and dressing up clothes.'

Rain lashed the car windscreen.

'It's a good place to go when the weather's bad,' the man said.

They parked in the multi-storey next to the council offices and the man got Jude's buggy out of the boot. Caz wheeled it into the building where her key worker was waiting. She asked Caz how she was doing.

When Caz didn't reply, the woman answered for her, 'We're doing well, thanks.'

The woman told Caz's key worker they were planning to do something nice afterwards. The key worker led them upstairs and showed them to some chairs lining a corridor. They sat next to one another in a row and waited for Luke to arrive.

Caz sensed him the moment he entered the building. She had seen a programme about dogs who know when their masters are coming home, even if their office is miles away. When he walked down the corridor, she knew it was him, even though she didn't look up, even though she kept her eyes on the door to the family room.

His social worker made him fill out some forms. Caz didn't look at him. She heard him say hello to Jude and call him 'little man'.

'Let me take you to a café,' the woman whispered in her ear. 'You don't have to be here.'

The woman was so close, Caz could smell her shampoo. She shut her eyes tight and kept them shut. Light splintered through her eyelids like the insides of a diamond. She tried to think about the fireflies she had seen in Corfu. She heard the squeak of the buggy wheels as the social worker took her child inside the family room. She felt someone take her elbow and lift her to her feet. She allowed herself to be led along the corridor. Outside, rain smacked her face and she felt the grip tighten on her arm.

She opened her eyes as the woman led her across the city square. Caz pulled her arm away. They were standing in front of a huge glass building. Its automatic door opened with a hiss.

'The library,' the woman said. 'We can wait in here.'

Caz took a step back and the automatic door shut again. In its mirrored surface, spattered with rain, she saw a young woman in a white puffer jacket and an older woman in a cagoule.

Caz turned and ran. The woman didn't follow her. When Luke's time was up, he would come out of the family room and she would look at him. He would call Jude 'little man' and the light would catch his diamond stud. They were in this story together. It would never end.

Carnival

IT WAS STILL DARK. The birds weren't awake yet. Cassie crept into her brother's room, using her phone to light her way to the wardrobe. Ryan stirred in his bed as she swept her beam of light over the clothes inside.

'What's the time?' he mumbled.

'Time to wake up,' she said, as she slipped one of his shirts off its hanger and held its sleeve along her arm. It would fit her, she had known it would, without her even having to roll up the cuffs. Ryan wouldn't miss it—he didn't wear shirts now he was working with their father. Cassie tiptoed out of the room and crossed the landing to lay the shirt on her bed, before heading downstairs to the kitchen.

'Morning, princess.' Her father was eating his breakfast and reading something on his phone. 'Ready for the rat race?' he asked, but he didn't look up from his phone when he spoke.

Hot water creaked in the pipes. Clothes were drying on the airer next to the boiler. Cassie spotted a pair of her brother's jeans. She hung them on the banister to take upstairs with her.

'Big fuss over nothing,' her father said, spooning cereal into his mouth. 'This business with the fans.'

A football shirt hung over the back of each dining chair. A pot of black face paint sat on the kitchen counter.

'It's tradition, that's all it is,' he said.

Cassie fetched a cup and a bowl from the cupboard. She filled the bowl with hot water. Upstairs, Ryan's phone barked like a dog.

Cassie's mother came in from her night shift. 'Are you not dressed yet?' she asked Cassie.

Cassie's father stood up from the table and began collecting his tools that were stacked in the lean-to off the kitchen.

'Let's go, boy!' he yelled up the stairs.

'How was work?' Cassie asked her mother.

'Oh, you know,' her mother said, slotting a piece of bread into the toaster. 'Ready for my bed.'

Cassie opened the freezer and took out a dead baby mouse.

'Koffi's injured,' Ryan said, entering the room.

'Fucking joke,' their father said.

Cassie dropped the mouse into the cup, placed the cup in the bowl of hot water, then carried it carefully upstairs.

Her brother's shirt lay on her bed, with the family cat asleep on top of it. She picked up a five-kilo hand weight and whisper-counted ten bicep curls while she waited for the mouse to thaw. Then she eased the shirt out from underneath the cat and put it on. It was warm from the small furry body.

Outside, Ryan and their father were loading tools into the van, their feet crunching on the gravel. Cassie heard the slide of the van doors, and the sputter of its engine. She listened to the beep of the warning signal as her father reversed on to the road. She pulled on Ryan's jeans, which were stiff from the wash and too big around the waist. She threaded a belt through the loops, while the cat rubbed itself against her legs, purring and meowing.

'Hush now,' she told it. 'I'll feed you in a minute.'

She picked up her grandmother's gold watch, stretching it as she put it over her wrist, but then she took it off again and lay it back down among the toiletries and hair elastics on the top of her chest of drawers. She tweezered the baby mouse, but Coral showed no interest as she dangled it into the vivarium. The snake's beautiful orange skin looked less glossy this morning—she was about to shed. Cassie closed the vivarium lid. In the room next door, her parents' mattress creaked as her mother got into bed.

Cassie tinkled some cat biscuits into a bowl and left the house. She felt a little self-conscious waiting at the bus stop in her brother's clothes, and found herself standing differently, her feet wider, her hands shoved deep inside his pockets. No one paid her any attention. When the bus came it was crammed with students.

'Can you move down, please?' she asked a young guy wearing headphones and a Supreme hoodie. The boy glanced at her but didn't budge.

'Move down the bus, please,' said the driver, and people shuffled deeper inside.

The guy in the hoodie moved to one side so Cassie could fit next to him. She could smell his deodorant. The bus started moving and swaying on its journey, passing traffic that had come to a halt in the other lanes, and sailing past crowded bus stops, its *Sorry I'm Not in Service* sign illuminated. Cyclists pedalled along in the bike lane, their hands and faces pink with cold. Cassie looked out for her line manager, Dan, who cycled in to work every day. Today's fundraiser was to come to work dressed as your boss, but she didn't look anything like him. What she really needed was a bike helmet.

At the end of the road leading to the football stadium, metal barricades lay in piles, waiting to be erected. Big crowds were expected for the Monday-night match. The bus trundled past the park and Cassie caught a glimpse of the river as they headed towards the outskirts of town.

Students spilled off the bus at the university stop. Cassie followed them as they snaked towards lecture theatres and laboratories. She headed to the library, an old red-brick building that had been closed for a year for renovations. It had re-opened recently and now featured a new glass extension. Cassie swiped her ID card at the barriers, nodded to the security guy on the front desk, and continued on her way to the library management suite.

Her colleagues in Research Support looked like they were celebrating a hen party. Ella and Chinwe were wearing pink feather boas, and oversized sunglasses in the shape of flamingos, miniature bride's veils pinned in their hair.

'Are they saying I'm married to my job, or what?' Jane called out, as Cassie passed through their department.

'I can't see a thing in these,' Ella said, taking off the sun-glasses and whizzing her wheely chair away from the desk. She ran to catch up with her friend. 'Good weekend?' she asked, patting her hair and adjusting the tiny veil.

'Quiet,' Cassie said.

'Are you meant to be Dan?'

'Yeah.'

'You should have asked me to borrow something,' Ella said. 'See Jane lent me her Oscars?' She stopped to waggle a foot, showing off the designer shoes her boss had loaned her for the day.

'Very nice,' Cassie said.

'Fucking killing me,' Ella said. 'Chinwe's are even higher.'

They arrived in Archives, and Ella gave Cassie a little wave as she headed into Dan's office, knocking on his door, but not waiting for an answer before she went in. She kicked up a heel as she disappeared inside, to show Cassie she knew she was watching. She and Ella had begun working at the library at the same time, starting as student interns before they were both offered staff contracts. Now, Ella was training as a Research Support librarian and going out with the head of Digital Collections. Cassie could hear her laughing behind his office door.

She switched on her computer and opened her emails, trawling through the ones from management she could safely delete, flagging ones with loan requests to read properly later.

Dan's office door opened.

'See you later, hon,' Ella called out, as she strode towards the lifts.

Cassie wasn't sure if she meant her or Dan.

'Thinks she's the bee's knees, doesn't she?' said a voice.

Cassie stood up and leaned over the divider separating her desk from Sonya's.

'I didn't know you were in,' Cassie said.

'There's football tonight, isn't there? Been here since eight.'

'You didn't feel like dressing up?' Cassie asked.

Sonya was wearing her usual uniform of black jeans and pussy-bow blouse. Her Michael Kors handbag sat on its own chair next to her. She dug inside it and brought out a lip gloss. Cassie watched her sweep the little applicator stick back and forth over her mouth.

'I'll put five pounds in the pot anyway,' Sonya said in between sweeps, 'if that's what you're worried about.'

'I'm not worried,' Cassie said.

It had been Ella's idea to turn the world upside down for a day, following the mediaeval tradition of carnival, where servants impersonated their masters for twenty-four hours. She had proposed it at a team meeting when they were both working for Dan and had been discussing fundraising ideas. Money was needed if the library was to hang on to valuable archives, which university management were threatening to sell off.

Dan's office door opened.

'All good, ladies?' Dan said. He gripped the top of the door frame and hoisted his body up, exposing the waistband of his Calvins. He pointed his feet, extended his legs in front of him, and puffing noisily, he performed a few pull-ups before jerking forwards and landing on the floor. He darted one hand to the front of his trousers, rearranging himself, before asking if they had both had a good weekend.

'Yes, thanks,' Cassie said.

'Are you meant to be me?' he asked, approaching her desk.

'Yes,' she said.

'Stand up, let's have a look at you.'

Cassie stood up. Behind the divider, she heard Sonya's fingers stop tapping on her keyboard.

'Not really my style,' Dan said.

Her brother's jeans were bunched around her waist where she had gathered them in with her belt. She should have asked Ella to get her something of Dan's so she could have surprised him with her outfit. Truth was, she was worried Ella would suggest wearing a pair of his Calvins. When they first started working at the library, they used to joke about Dan-the-man's underwear and how hot he was. A day when they spotted his Calvins was known between them as a 'Good Day'. They would ask each other if they were having a good day, or if it had been a 'Good Day', and if the other answered that yes, they were having a 'Good Day', the two of them knew what that meant. Sonya used to tell them they were being childish, even though she had no idea what their code meant. Now Ella was going out with him, it was kind of awkward.

'She needs a bike helmet,' Sonya said, wheeling her chair out from behind her desk. Her lips were very shiny.

'Excellent idea!' Dan said.

He went inside his office and unhooked his bike helmet from the back of his door with a clatter.

'Thanks a lot,' Cassie said.

'You're welcome,' Sonya said, disappearing behind her desk once more.

Dan came out of his office holding the helmet out towards Cassie. He put it on her head and fastened the strap under her chin. He was so close she could smell his aftershave, citrussy and astringent.

'Have you had coffee yet?' he asked.

'No,' she said, keeping her eyes fixed on the carpet. 'Do you want one?'

'Star woman,' he said, flashing his sexy smile.

In the staff kitchen, Cassie threw away old coffee grounds and slotted a new filter into the machine. While she waited for the water to heat, she studied the poster Ella had made, which was pinned to the noticeboard.

MONTHLY FUNDRAISER
Pay £5 to spend the day bossing your boss!
All money raised will go to charity!

The image on the poster was a 1950s fashion illustration of a woman in a trouser suit striding across the page at an angle. Cassie crouched down to tuck her right trouser leg into her sock. Sometimes Dan would forget to untuck his when he got off his bike in the morning. In the early days, she and Ella would bet each other how long it would take him to remember, and the loser would have to buy the winner a Danish.

She delivered his coffee.

'Thanks, mate,' he said, glancing up from his computer.

She saw him notice the sock.

'One more thing,' he said, as she reached the door. He removed a hi-vis tabard from the back of his chair and came around the front of his desk, holding it out for her. Cassie slipped her arms obediently inside. 'That's more like it,' he said.

It was her turn to collect the money people were donating.

'Don't tell me—Danny in Digital, right?' one of the post-room guys said, when she went down to the basement.

Cassie shoved her hand down the front of her trousers and the post-room guy laughed.

'Ha! Very good,' he said. 'Rearranging the crown jewels!'

He was wearing lipstick and eye make-up, and his colleague had two pink balloons stuffed down the front of his shirt.

'Bit less glam than your last costume.'

She guessed he was talking about the previous fundraiser, with its superhero theme. Cassie had come as Wonder Woman, which seemed to surprise people. Ella told her she looked fit that day.

She took off the bike helmet and held it out for his money.

'We thought you were a bit of a mouse before that,' he said, dropping a tenner into the helmet. 'That's for both of us,' he explained, indicating his colleague with a nod of his head.

'It's always the quiet ones,' the other guy said, grinning.

She spent the rest of the day answering loan requests, and ate lunch at her desk, listening to Sonya munching a packet of crisps. When Dan left the office, she wondered if he was meeting Ella for a sandwich at the café where they used to go when they were interns.

At the end of the afternoon, as the sun began to dip behind the buildings, Cassie saw the floodlights come on at the football stadium across the way. She took off Dan's hi-vis jacket and went to return his bike helmet, stuffed with five-pound notes.

'I wanted to give you back your things,' she said, and held out the bike helmet full of cash.

'Just get me an envelope from that cupboard, could you?' he said.

She opened the door to the stationery store, as Dan stood up from his desk.

'I think we raised even more money than last month,' she said, but he didn't answer. She felt his hands on her waist as he bundled her inside the cupboard and shut the door. 'Dan?'

It was dark inside the cupboard. She tried to open the door, but he was pressed up against it. She heard him turn the lock.

'Dan? Let me out.'

Fumbling for the handle, she pressed it up and down, but it was useless.

'Can you open the door, please?'

There was no answer. She could sense him on the other

side of the cheap laminate. She felt around for a light switch, running her fingers over the smooth walls.

'Dan?'

She couldn't hear anything and she couldn't see anything, not even her own hand in front of her face as she held it up. She covered her eyes with both hands, concentrating on breathing slowly and steadily. She couldn't remember if Sonya was still at her desk, or if she had already gone home. Had she left early because of match-day traffic?

Cassie tapped on the door.

'Dan?'

She took deep breaths, concentrating on her out-breath like her mum had taught Ryan to do when he was having a panic attack.

'Dan?' she said, clearing her throat and trying to sound firm. 'I need to go now, please.'

She heard his voice distantly. He was talking to Sonya as she packed up her things.

'Hello?' she cried out, raising her voice a little.

Nothing.

She pressed her ear to the door. Her phone was in her desk drawer, otherwise she could text Ella. What would she write: *Pls help. Your bf has locked me in a cupboard*?

She heard Sonya leave and now she concentrated on the silence, trying to detect if Dan had come back into his office. There was no sound, just her own ragged breathing. If she shouted loud enough somebody might hear—a cleaner or a security guard, or one of the post-room guys as they wheeled their trolley up and down. But she didn't want to make a fuss.

As her eyes adjusted to the dark, pale squares of paper piled up on the shelves became visible and she tried to pretend she was in a cave, like a member of some ancient tribe. A soft cave, with papery smells and a temperature almost the same as her own body. A safe haven.

She slid down the wall, sitting on the floor and wrapping her arms around her knees, rubbing the denim of her brother's trousers between her fingers. She untucked her sock. Was Dan planning to lock her in here overnight? She would have to empty one of the cardboard boxes of printer paper and use it as a toilet. She felt a sudden pang in her bowels. He would have to let her out in the morning—and then what? They would pretend nothing had happened. What would she do with her toilet box? She would have to hide it behind the shelving and dispose of it at lunchtime. She reached out and blindly shuffled items around on the shelf to make room for hiding any temporary toilet she might need to use.

'Doing a bit of tidying up?'

Dan. His voice sounded normal.

Cassie scrambled to her feet. 'Thought I may as well,' she said, trying to keep her tone light. 'Can you let me out now, please?'

Silence.

Maybe she had overreacted. She'd only been locked in for, like, ten minutes and she was busy planning how she'd survive the night! She leaned her forehead against the door.

'Dan?'

She started counting so she could estimate the number of minutes going by, whispering the numbers so she could keep track. Was that a vacuum she could hear? She could shout for the cleaners. If Dan left, one of them would have a master key. At least she wouldn't be here all night. Then she remembered the memo from management that had gone round, explaining that cleaning staff would only clean offices once a fortnight now. She wasn't sure if it was a vacuum she could hear. She knocked on the door. She could hear drumming coming from somewhere. Or was it Dan, sitting behind his desk only feet away, drumming his fingers? The thought that he was waiting until they were the only people left in the building made her bowels twinge again. She felt around for a weapon among the paper and pen supplies, weighing a stapler to feel how heavy it was, before she found a pair of scissors to stab the air.

'Are you coming?'

Ella's voice.

'Ella?' Cassie rapped loudly on the cupboard door.

'What was that?'

'Ella, it's me—Cass.'

There was a brief pause and a rustle before the handle twisted and the cupboard door opened. Ella stood in front of her.

'Open Sesame!' Dan said, behind her.

He was smiling.

Ella was talking to her, but Cassie walked past her and out of Dan's office. She slung down the scissors and scooped up her phone and bag from her desk. She kept walking.

'Not funny, Danny,' she heard her friend say behind her.

In Research Support, all the desks were empty, everyone had gone home early because of the match. Ella's pink feather boa was still draped over her computer. A security guard nodded at Cassie as she left the building. Outside, it was chilly and a smell of fried onions filled the air. Barricades had been set up along the roads and pavements, funnelling the crowds heading to the match. She checked her phone. There was a text from her mum asking if she wanted to eat before the game and a flurry of messages from Ella.

did it to me 2

office tradition :(

supposedly it means ur one of us now
c u tomorrow

Roads to the stadium were closed, there were no buses. Cassie began walking against the flow of the fans. Children and adults wore football shirts and plastic necklaces in the shape of bones. 'Sav-ag-es!' they chanted. 'Sav-ag-es!' Many of them had blackened their faces. Cassie looked out for her mum and dad and Ryan among the crowd, as she began to walk home.

The house was empty when she let herself in. Clothes still hung on the airer and her football shirt lay draped over the back of a kitchen chair. The cat trotted up, meowing a greeting. On the counter, a used make-up sponge lay next to the pot of face paint. Cassie took the lid off and drew her fingers across the sticky black substance. The cat weaved in and out of her legs, wanting her to feed it, or pet it. She ignored it, standing at the sink in her brother's clothes, looking out of the window and listening to the distant drums. She dragged her stained fingers across her face, streaking her cheeks like a warrior's.

She-Clown

Charlie parked her car outside the house. The arrangement of the upper windows and front door of the building gave it a quizzical expression. 'What are you doing here?' it seemed to ask.

'I'm She-Clown,' Charlie said, out loud, practising the voice she would use when she greeted today's customer.

She checked her make-up in the rear-view mirror. The eyelashes she had drawn around her eyes looked like dark rays around two dark suns.

She twisted the mirror away from her and smoothed the velvet of her costume, feeling the resistance of the fabric, its fibres moving backwards and forwards under her fingertips as she stroked it one way and then the other—from smooth to rough, then rough to smooth. She opened the glove compartment and took out a handful of balloons, stuffing them in the pocket of her pantaloons. Then she pulled out a box of condoms and slid one inside her top pocket.

Her bowler hat and patchwork coat lay on the back seat. She got out of the car and put on the coat, even though the afternoon was sultry. She placed the bowler hat on her head, pulling its elastic strap under her chin as she turned towards the house.

Two pink balloons were pinned to the front door. Charlie banged the knocker and waited. She could hear music and voices from inside. She knocked again.

'You must be the magician lady,' said the woman who opened the door. She wore a tight-fitting cream dress, and thin gold bangles on each wrist. Identical twin girls stood either side of her in the doorway, wearing matching T-shirts decorated with sequinned butterflies.

'I'm She-Clown,' Charlie said.

The woman invited her inside the house. The girls ran ahead of them down the hallway.

Music was playing in a bright, modern kitchen that looked out on to a garden. A woman also wearing a cream outfit, but with strappy sandals, was talking in a loud voice. 'Men have to be managed,' she was saying. 'Like farm animals!'

'You probably know half the people here,' the mother said, turning to Charlie, and it was true that Charlie did recognise some of the faces. One of the men had sat in her car. She had given him a blowjob. She recognised his moccasin shoes. Another man, in a pink Ralph Lauren shirt, had fucked her in a laundry room among mountain bikes and drying washing while his wife gave out party bags.

'My stuff's in the car,' Charlie said, raising her voice slightly, so she could make herself heard above the music. 'Is it okay if I leave the front door open?'

'Oh no, don't do that. Tony will give you a hand,' the twins' mother said, and she rapped on the window, getting the attention of a bearded man in the garden, who was standing next to a trampoline.

'Yes, Tony will give you a hand!' the loud woman said, and she laughed, leaning her whole body against her friend before tipping herself upright again.

'I can manage,' Charlie said.

But the bearded man was moving through the garden, making his way towards the kitchen door.

'No double dipping,' the mother told her friend, who took a carrot stick from a plate and bit into it.

'What's wrong with double dipping?' the loud woman asked, lifting the carrot high above her head then plunging it exaggeratedly into a dish of guacamole.

'Double dipper! Double dipper!' another guest yelled.

The bearded man came indoors.

'This is the She-Clown,' the mother told him.

'She Clam?'

'She-Clown,' the mother corrected. She opened the fridge and took out a bottle of wine.

'Pleased to meet you,' the bearded man said to Charlie.

'She needs your help,' the mother said, gathering a bouquet of wine glasses, holding them upside down by their stems.

'I don't really,' Charlie said.

A woman standing next to her had the hem of Charlie's coat in her hands. 'Did you make your outfit?' she asked. Like the twins' mother and her friend, she was wearing cream.

'Yes,' Charlie said. 'Smell my flower.'

The woman let the coat hem fall from her fingers and moved her face close to the plastic flower in Charlie's buttonhole. With a swift squirt, an arc of water sprinkled into the air.

'Missed!' the woman said, stepping backwards on her high heels.

Outside, the twins bounced on the trampoline, their hair flying.

Away from the noise of the party, the street was quiet. Charlie lifted her oversized suitcase out of the boot of her car and hooked her hula hoop over her shoulder. The bearded man, who Charlie presumed was the twins' father, took hold of her folding table and they carried her things back to the house. He leaned the table against his body while he fitted his key in the lock. She wondered if it was him who had blown up the balloons pinned to the door.

The mother and her guests watched Charlie as she moved through the kitchen and out into the garden, where the twins' father unfolded the table legs. Charlie spread her embroidered tablecloth, poured bubble mixture into her bucket, and laid out her giant wand, her spinning plates and sticks.

'I'm ready,' she said, and the father called to the trampolining girls that the magic was about to start.

The twins leaped off the trampoline and ran around the garden while he called for them to come and sit down. Their friends gave chase, spilling and falling over one another, snatching leaves off trees. An older girl asked if she had to watch the show. The twins' father told her, in a low voice, that it would be nice if she would, please, and to put away her phone. At last, the twins threw themselves on to the grass, reaching up for the cups of apple juice their father handed them.

Two of the girls' friends said they had a trick they wanted to show him.

'Go on, then,' he said.

'It's called the tank,' one of them said, and their friends groaned, complaining that all of them knew how to do the tank—they had learned it at gymnastics. Undeterred, the first girl lay on her back and lifted her feet in the air. Her friend caught hold of her ankles and then tipped herself forwards, rolling head over heels between her friend's legs, taking her friend with her because she kept hold of her ankles. Over and over they went, keeping hold of one another and moving around the garden as one. The father laughed and told the girls they looked nothing like a tank.

'Do we get a prize?' one of the girls asked, but there were no prizes, he told them, only magic.

It was time to start the show. Charlie banged her gong and blew her kazoo.

She began with the ping-pong ball trick, and when the girls demanded to know how the balls appeared under their cups, she told them a magician never reveals her technique. They shouted back that she wasn't a real magician. By way of an answer she juggled the ping-pong balls then threw them into the girls' upheld cups, aiming carefully.

'That's not magic!' the girls cried.

'No?' she said, cocking her head. 'What is it then?'

'It's sport,' the older girl said.

'It's sport,' chorused the younger girls.

'It's harder than you think,' their father told them. 'To get every one of those balls in every cup.'

He bent to pick up a ball and have a go himself, and Charlie noticed a line of pale skin at the nape of his neck where his tan ended before his T-shirt began.

She handed out sticks to each of the guests and set plates spinning on them, but the older girl wouldn't hold hers, so Charlie offered it to the father instead and he took it. Then she pulled a tutu on over her velvet pantaloons and he held the fishing rod she gave him, with a paper bird fastened to its line, high above his head. She twirled round and around, underneath the fishing rod, chasing the bird.

'That's not magic,' the twins cried, clutching each other in delight. 'That's ballet!'

She fell inside her oversized suitcase, and the girls shrieked with laughter to see her feet in their clown shoes waving about. Charlie stared at her rainbow shoelaces waggling against the sky. In the kitchen, she could hear the twins' mother and her friends laughing and drinking wine. Laying where she was, Charlie reached inside her pocket and fished out a balloon. She blew into it and it arched into the sky in front of her. She made a show of struggling out of the suitcase, coming to stand once more in front of her audience. They screamed and clamped their hands over their ears every time she tugged the balloon, threatening to make it pop. She made a butterfly for each birthday girl, handing them a Sharpie to draw eyes and a mouth on its squeaky pink face. Then she twisted two balloons together to make a flower, which she presented to the girls' father, with a bow.

'Very clever,' he said.

She finished with bubbles, dipping her gigantic wand into the bucket of bubble mixture and waving it back and forth to waft them over the fence into a neighbour's garden. Their soft bobbing motion sent the children into a kind of trance. She bowed once, twice, and then, turning around, she bowed a third time—showing them the word *End*, stitched on the seat of her velvet trousers.

She felt the twins' father watching her as she put the lid on the bucket of bubble mixture and folded away her picnic table. He was still holding the balloon flower she had given him.

'I like my flower,' he said. 'Where did you learn to do that?'

'YouTube,' she said.

It wasn't true. Dad had made her a balloon animal every birthday until she got too old for balloons and he left.

'She-Clown's going, everyone!' the twins' mother cried, as Charlie and the twins' father passed back through the kitchen. She waved her wine glass in the air. 'Bye-bye, She-Clown!'

'Bye-bye, Tony,' someone said.

'We paid you when we booked, right?' the mother said, following them to the front door.

'Just the deposit,' Charlie told her.

'Oh,' the twins' mother looked at their father, who laughed and put down the folding table to dig inside his jeans pocket.

'How much?' he asked.

The mother looked at Charlie. 'Remind me?'

'Seventy-five, please,' Charlie said.

'Seventy-five,' the mother said, moving closer to her husband as he counted out the money.

He handed the notes to Charlie. They were warm from his body.

'I thought your name was She Clam, earlier,' he said, as he led the way down the tiled path.

'She-Clown.'

She glanced back at the house as she opened the boot of her car. The twins' mother stood watching them from the doorway. Sometimes the man would suggest sitting in the car with her, with the excuse of escaping party mayhem.

'There's no difference between male and female clams, did you know that?' he said. 'No difference in colour, or markings, or mating behaviour. So only the clam knows who's who and what's what.'

He slid the picnic table inside the car and took the suitcase from her, wedging it in next to the table. Charlie noticed, once more, the place where his tan ended on the back of his neck. She smoothed the velvet of her costume this way and that, stroking it from smooth to rough, then rough to smooth. He shut the boot, and they stood opposite one another.

'I really enjoyed your show,' he said.

Charlie looked at the ground, where a dandelion grew in a crack in the pavement. 'Thanks.'

'We're separated, my wife and I,' he said. 'We're not together, if you see what I mean.'

Here we go, she thought. She took off her bowler hat, rubbing the place on her cheek where the elastic had pressed into her skin.

'Well, I'd better get back to the party,' he said.

He waited while she got into her car and started the engine. As she pulled away from the kerb, he ducked down to smile at her through the window. She drove a short distance to the junction at the end of the road, and when she looked in her rear-view mirror, he had gone into the house, disappearing inside its funny face.

Benediction

TOMMY'S PLACE was a shithole. The kitchen was so small and cramped, two people had to stand side by side to fit inside it. The tiny living room was filled with a flesh-coloured mock-leather sofa. The bathroom walls were speckled with mould. A sign over the back door read: *Follow your heart. If you can't follow your heart, follow your cock.* Tommy had done both. He had moved out to live with his boyfriend with three months of his tenancy left. He said we could renew it in his name, if we wanted. If we could afford it.

A spider scuttled out of the sink plughole when I turned on the tap. It ran up the side of the sink and fell down again. I managed to scoop it out.

'Oi!' Ayesha yelled.

She was in the bath, standing behind a shower curtain printed with a map of the world. The Pacific Ocean was mildewed where it was stuck against the tiles. I spat out toothpaste and turned off the tap. The shower started up again.

I rattled the curtain along the rail on its cheap plastic fittings and climbed in next to her. 'Bit different to the bucket shower, eh,' I said.

I gave her a peck with my minty mouth, but the flow of water was puny and there wasn't enough room for two, so she got out. I heard her drying herself on the other side of the mouldy curtain.

It seemed a shame to wash away skin cells that had grown during our trip, but my feet were filthy and my hair was sticky with salt, so I stood under the tepid sprinkle and got on with it. Welcome home.

In the kitchen, we sat at the small Formica table waiting for the washing machine to complete its cycle so we could take our clothes to the launderette for drying. I cut my toenails with some nail clippers I found in an ashtray next to the kettle.

Our bodies looked a different colour in England.

'Like my bikini?' I asked, standing up to show her my pale breasts and the mark where my pants had been.

She picked up her watch from the table.

'Why are you in a mood?' I asked, but she just shrugged.

I asked her the time—not because I wanted to know, just for something to say. When she told me it was twelve, I reminded her it would be seven on Bottle Beach, where we'd been only two nights ago. She fastened her watch around her wrist.

'Greenwich Mean Time feels mean alright,' I said. 'We should have stayed.'

She didn't say anything. I knew she felt an urgency to get on with our lives. She had said as much. 'Isn't *this* getting on with our lives?' I had asked her, as we lay side by side on warm sand. 'What is there to get on with?'

She went quiet on me, and she had been quiet ever since.

I watched her hands as she arranged some loose change on the table top into small piles around a pepper grinder. The coins were Thai baht and the pepper grinder was in the shape of a man's muscly torso, wearing a stripy sailor's top and neckerchief. The washing machine whirred. I went into the bedroom and pulled on pants, jeans, sweatshirt, and a pair of tube socks, then squeezed my feet into my old Vans. It felt weird to be wearing proper shoes after weeks of living in flip-flops. When I came back down, she was still sitting at the table. I opened the fridge, but the shelves were empty, apart from half an egg sandwich we bought on the way home from the airport.

'Want some?' I held out the sandwich but she waved it away. I chucked it in the bin. 'Let's do this thing then,' I said, clapping my hands.

'What about the washing?'

'Take it later, when we come back. Ready?'

'Ready,' she said.

We made our way down an alleyway that ran along the back of the houses.

'Don't step in that,' I said, pointing out a puddle of puke outside the back gate. Someone had had a good Friday night.

The alley was so narrow we had to walk one behind the other. I was in front.

'Another one, whoah!' I pointed out a second splatter of sick and checked to see she was following me. I'd forgotten what she looked like in proper clothes, after months of wearing a sarong. I fancied her even more, if that was possible.

On the main road, buses, cars and trucks thundered past, whipping her hair into my face. An old woman at the bus stop told us not to bother reading the timetable.

'Worse than useless,' she said. 'They make it up as they go along.'

I lifted Ayesha's wrist to check her watch.

'You can check the time all you want, young man, won't make the bus come any sooner.'

'I'm not a man,' I said, but the old woman couldn't hear me above the noise of the traffic.

'What's that?' she said, jutting her chin forwards and squinting her crinkled up eyes at me.

I glanced at Ayesha but she was staring into the traffic.

'I said, I'm not a man,' I shouted.

The old woman shrugged. Welcome home.

The bus was full of strangers. Most of our uni mates were living back with their parents, or like Tommy, they had moved on. The university term hadn't started yet and there were *To Let* signs on all the student houses on the ring road.

We got off the bus outside the supermarket entrance. Neither of us had a pound coin for the trolley. I went to ask a woman at the Customer Service counter for change and she told me free eye tests were available in-store today. A temporary opticians had been set up in a dark-green gazebo behind the tills. The gazebo was decorated with cardboard bunting in the shape of spectacles, reminding me of the prayer flags around the temples we visited in Nepal, except not.

I slotted a pound into the metal trolley and wheeled it over to where Ayesha was waiting for me in the fruit and veg aisle.

'I don't think I can do this,' she said, dragging her feet.

'We need to eat, come on.' I tossed the rucksack into the trolley. My Vans squeaked on the shiny supermarket floor.

Everything was clean and bright and neatly wrapped. Customers moved along, reaching products off the shelves as if they were sleepwalking. They moved around each other without touching.

'Fuck this,' Ayesha hissed. 'Everything's so expensive.'

We headed for the 'reduced goods'. I put a cauliflower in the trolley. It was going brown, but it would do for curry.

'I'm thinking I may need to get a proper job,' she said.

'Uh-huh.'

Carrots, onions, potatoes. We moved into refrigerated foods.

'I might do a year at college—get that teaching thing Sol told me about.'

I wasn't really listening. Standing next to the yoghurts it was fucking freezing. She wandered ahead, turning into the 'World Cuisine' aisle, and then she laid it on me.

'Could be time to put down some roots,' she said. 'Start thinking about babies?'

'What the fuck?'

'Just an idea,' she said, in a strange, light kind of voice.

I could tell she was concentrating on the packets of rice and noodles so she wouldn't have to meet my eye.

'Don't go all mushy on me, will you?' I said.

But she didn't answer. She took the trolley, wheeling it fast along to where the pasta was.

'There's so much of the world we still need to see,' I said, picking up a packet of Mexican wraps. The logo on the packaging was a moustachioed cartoon figure wearing a sombrero and marching around the edge of a globe.

'I think I might want a baby,' she said. The way she looked at me slayed me.

'What's brought this on?' I asked. My voice did a horrible wobble. 'You never said anything before.'

'I never felt like this before.'

She checked her watch, even though it was hours before she needed to be at the restaurant. There was a guy who did the washing up who fancied the pants off her. What was his name? Funny name. All you have to do is say the word, he told her before we left. We laughed about it. Shippy, that was his name. He was in love with her.

We did the rest of the shop in a kind of daze. When we got to the tills, I saw Ayesha clock a family whose little boy was running around in a superhero costume.

'Want to have a go?' The cashier pointed over her shoulder at the pop-up opticians. 'It's free. I had mine done yesterday—blind as a bat, I am! Had no idea.'

The boy in the superhero costume poked his sister with a loaf of French bread and she grabbed it and broke it in two. We packed our shopping into my rucksack and I paid with my credit card. Ayesha tried to get the sticky airport label off the shoulder strap, but it really needed a pair of scissors. The couple with the children wheeled their loaded trolley away, not noticing that their daughter was having a strop. She sat on the floor with her legs and arms crossed, head bowed. As we passed her, on our way to the pop-up optician's, she looked up to check where her family were, then scrambled to her feet and ran to catch up with them.

A woman in a trouser suit stood outside the optician's gazebo, announcing that this was where the eye examinations took place. Her name badge read *Amalie*.

'Appointments are fifteen minutes each,' she said, 'and this service is totally free of charge today.' Her blouse stretched taut across her breasts. 'Is it for yourself?' she asked me.

'Me, and my partner,' I said, nodding at Ayesha.

Amalie quickly lowered her eyes to a pile of forms on her clipboard. She licked her finger and separated two pages from the rest, handing one to each of us.

We sat down inside the gazebo, parking our rucksack and filling out our names, addresses and dates of birth. A man appeared from behind a maroon curtain. According to his name badge, this was Dharmit.

'The optician is ready for you now,' Amalie said. 'Who wants to go first?'

I followed Dharmit behind the curtain which Amalie held aside like a magician's assistant.

'Good day to you,' the optician said, bowing slightly.

The genteelness of his manner made me feel a bit tearful, to be honest, but I was worried he wouldn't be able to carry out the eye test if I was crying.

'Have a seat, Celia,' he said, gesturing for me to sit.

'Ci-ci,' I whispered. 'I prefer to be called Ci-ci.'

He gave an odd kind of grunt and asked if I had any problems with my eyesight.

'Not as far as I know.'

A chart was pinned to the back of the curtain.

A

O E

H L A

N T C O

H L A O T

N T L A O E

L N E T H O A

The optician took up a small metal instrument, like a miniature telescope, and placed it in front of my left eye. He swatted his tie out of the way and peered down the other end of the instrument.

'Look up, please,' he said.

I did as I was told.

'And down.'

He placed it in front of my right eye. Then he picked up a small torch and shone its beam straight into my eyeball. I felt the needle of light pierce me and I was reduced to a pinprick. Then he did the same with my left eye. Once more, the fine blade of light made a sliver out of me. I was a beam, a dot, a twinkle in my mother's eye. I thought about all the places I want to go. If Ayesha didn't want to come with me, I'd go on my own. I felt light-headed, as if I might pass out. My vision splintered into thousands of tiny mirrors, like the ones decorating the bedspread we bought in Rajasthan. What if I asked her to marry me, would that make a difference? Maybe it was commitment she wanted, not a baby. The optician gave me a pair of heavy goggles to wear.

'Better or worse?'

'Sorry?'

'Look at the chart, please—better or worse?'

'Er...I don't know.'

'No difference.'

The sudden flutter of his hands across my face made me shiver.

I caught the smell of something sweet and spicy—cinnamon? Cardamom? It made me think of a border crossing we did in India somewhere. I was tired from travelling overnight on a crowded train, but Ayesha was excited, watching the monkeys in the trees, laughing a lot and talking all the time.

Maybe we should have a baby. She would look so beautiful pregnant.

'Look at the screen, please.'

I tried to focus on the letters in front of me.

'Read me the third line from the top.'

'H, L, A.'

Helas could be a nice name for a girl. No, too sad. The optician slotted a different lens into the glasses.

'Better or worse?'

'Better.'

'Can you read the fourth line?'

'N, T, C, O.'

How about Nico? Pretty for a girl, or a boy.

The optician removed the glasses and picked up his torch, leaning forward to shine his light into my eyes once more. He lifted my right eyelid and then my left. His fingers were cool, but his breath was warm. Saliva gathered at the corners of my mouth as I surrendered to his touch.

A baby would be a fellow traveller, a companion to share experiences, not even someone to show the world, but another person to discover it with. And Ayesha as its mother. Who would be the father? There was my brother, of course, but he already had children of his own, and his annoying wife wouldn't agree to it. Shippy would be willing, sad bastard, or maybe Tommy? Or we could go for a donor. It was possible—anything was possible. Ayesha would have our baby and we would wrap it in an Indian shawl, pin a Thai wall hanging above its cot. Who knows, maybe I could provide a sibling, one day. We could discuss it on the way home.

Maybe I drifted off—the perfume I could smell, was it a sedative? I thought about Chloroform, about Rohypnol. I was wide awake again now. The optician stepped away, pausing for a moment before leaning close again. I held my breath, trying not to share the same oxygen as this man. The muscles in my chest strained with the effort, while the optician, seemingly unaware, leaned closer until his forehead was resting against mine. I could hear a faint whistling in his nostrils. My body stiffened as he moved his head side to side, his skull rolling against mine, the heat from his skin warming mine. I got ready to say something, like Ayesha did to that guy on the bus in Turkey, but Dharmit pulled away, straightening up and putting his torch in the top pocket of his jacket.

'Good,' he said, and took up the form I had filled in, writing something on it.

'How are my eyes?' I asked him.

'Perfect vision, Miss Ci-ci. Twenty-twenty, no problem.'

He held the curtain open for me and I stepped back into the waiting area.

'Everything okay?' Ayesha asked, when I emerged.

The supermarket lights were too bright. I felt weak and strangely shy.

'Kind of weird,' I said.

'Weird how?'

But I didn't have a chance to answer because it was her turn. Amalie ushered her through the curtain and I sat down on the plastic chair to plan our future. It was still warm from where she had been sitting.

The Poison Frog

EVEN THOUGH Charlotte was thirty years old, she still lived with her mother. They went everywhere together and were a familiar sight in their neighbourhood, walking arm in arm along the high street, or waiting at the bus stop in their macs.

'How are you ladies?' the local grocer would ask them, every time they went into his shop. 'Healthy, wealthy and wise?'

'Not so wealthy,' Charlotte's mother would answer, and Hassan always said he was sorry to hear that.

'We've only stopped off for a paper and my mints,' she told him today, when they called in on their way to the dentist.

'Low sugar,' Hassan said, folding the newspaper and placing the packet of mints neatly on top. 'You know how to look after yourself.'

'Well, if you get to my age and don't know that, well then,' said Charlotte's mother.

As they left the shop, Charlotte heard him say something in his own language. He had taught Charlotte a few words. She knew 'chehra' for 'face', and 'muhn' for 'mouth'. She tried to hold on to the brown of his eyes ('aankhaiyn') all the way to their appointment.

The dentist was used to Charlotte and her mother attending the surgery together. They had been going to her since Charlotte was a girl.

'Who's first?' she asked, and Charlotte and her mother looked at one another for a moment, each waiting for the other.

'Shall I?' Charlotte said.

Charlotte's mother followed her into the consulting room and sat on a chair while Charlotte settled herself on to the examination couch. The dentist flicked a switch on the wall, which set a miniature model train in motion. Its track ran around the perimeter of the room, guiding the train over a small humpbacked bridge and past a field of fake grass, dotted with sheep. In the corner of the room where her mother sat, the track climbed steeply to run overhead and across the top of the door. The train whizzed down an incline on the other side of the door and whistled through a miniature station, which was positioned opposite the examination couch so that patients could just detect a tiny businessman reading his newspaper on the platform.

'How are your teeth, Charlotte?' the dentist asked. 'Any problems I should know about?'

Charlotte couldn't speak with her mouth open and the dentist's gloved hands inside it.

'Guh,' she said.

'Very good,' murmured the dentist.

Then it was her mother's turn in the chair and they swapped places. Charlotte watched the miniature train, transfixed by the little lights inside its carriages.

'Any sore throat or coughing lately?' the dentist asked Charlotte's mother.

With her mouth still open, Charlotte's mother shook her head.

'No?' The dentist seemed surprised.

Charlotte's mother snapped her mouth shut and the dentist cocked her head, studying her for a moment.

'It's just—there seems to be...you have an obstruction in your throat. It could be something, or it could be nothing, but I think I'll refer you to a specialist...just to be safe.'

The train rattled along its track. Charlotte watched it disappear behind the dentist and emerge on the other side. It carried on its way, relentless.

'You have been coughing lately,' Charlotte said to her mother, once they were outside.

'What?'

'Coughing—I hear you in the mornings sometimes.'

'Parky, isn't it?' her mother said, drawing her coat around her. 'Brass monkeys.'

When they got home a postcard had arrived saying there was a parcel. Charlotte slipped her shoes back on and went to collect it. Hassan's sister, Noor, was serving. She wore a lilac tunic, with loose cotton trousers to match. The material of her outfit was shot through with silver thread that caught the light from the overhead fluorescent strip. She handed Charlotte the parcel and Charlotte took it home.

Inside the package was a new coat she had ordered from her mother's catalogue—black wool, with tiny tufts of white in the weave, like stars in a night sky.

'Try it on then,' her mother said, and they went into her bedroom together to examine it in the full-length mirror.

'I like it,' Charlotte said, studying her reflection and trying to avoid the gaze of her mother's doll collection. Around twenty of them were arranged along a shelf, and a few more sat on a dressing table under the window. She turned sideways to show how the coat nipped in at the waist. 'It's lined, too—look.' She held the coat open to show her mother.

'Looks tarty,' her mother said. 'Something plainer would be better.'

The next morning Charlotte heard her mother coughing. She knocked on her bedroom door and opened it a crack. The room was dark and smelled of cheese. Her mother was sitting up in bed.

'Shall I open the curtains?' Charlotte asked.

She crossed the room, feeling the eyes of her mother's dolls on her. They had wide-open eyes, pink cheeks and rosebud lips. Dressed in lace and velvet Victorian-style outfits, their legs stuck out stiffly from beneath their skirts.

'Is your throat sore?' Charlotte asked her mother, tugging the curtains open.

'I can't seem to get rid of this blasted frog.'

'The dentist asked if you've had a cough or a sore throat, didn't she?'

'I've looked after my skin,' her mother said, pulling on the white cotton gloves she wore for cleansing and moisturising. 'One thing you can't accuse me of, one thing no one can accuse me of, is not having looked after my skin.'

She reached for a pot of cold cream on her bedside table.

'I'm glad we're getting an appointment with the specialist,' Charlotte said.

The Poison Frog

'Lot of fuss,' was her mother's reply, as she closed her eyes and dabbed cream on her face and neck with little white paws. 'We should think about going elsewhere—I mean, if she thinks a train set is going to help! It doesn't exactly inspire confidence, does it?'

Charlotte noticed that the coat she had bought had been repackaged and was waiting on her mother's dressing table, ready to be sent back.

'You really should cleanse, Charlotte,' her mother said, tipping her head back and massaging the cream around her throat in a series of deft, upward strokes. 'Combination skin like yours—it's a worry.'

In the weeks that followed, Charlotte's mother's neck began to swell and she took to wearing a silk scarf knotted around her throat, even though she insisted the lump was nothing. But it wasn't nothing, the specialist said, when they visited the hospital a month later. It was something.

'Something living,' he said, as he shone a small torch inside Charlotte's mother's mouth.

'Something living?' Charlotte asked. She wasn't certain she had heard the doctor correctly. He was very handsome, wearing a pink shirt and smart shoes.

'That's right,' the doctor said, taking a step back to survey Charlotte and her mother. He gave a little chuckle as he replaced his torch in the breast pocket of his shirt. 'A frog, specifically.' He gave another little chuckle and explained that he didn't like to use the word 'parasite', as the frog was a creature capable of surviving outside its host organism. 'We can give you a scan,' he continued. 'But you'd have to wait for that. There's another test we can do here today, if you'd like?'

Charlotte's mother waved her hand at the doctor, telling him she didn't give a hoot.

'Well, in that case,' the doctor said, and he whipped out a pair of latex gloves from a box on his desk and put them on. He leaned down to open a small fridge beside the desk. As well as rows of vials and bottles, the fridge contained a Tupperware box. The doctor lifted the lid off the box and peeled away a layer of bread from a sandwich to reveal some lettuce.

'Bear with me,' he said, as he tore off a small piece of lettuce and replaced the lunchbox in the fridge. The doctor took a travel sewing kit from his desk drawer, and Charlotte and her mother watched as he threaded a needle and pierced the piece of lettuce with it, securing it to the thread.

'Would you mind swallowing this?' he asked, holding out the piece of lettuce to Charlotte's mother.

'Don't mind if I do,' she croaked. She took the piece of lettuce and swallowed it whole, while the doctor held on to the thread, letting it out a little so its length slackened between them.

'Now, let's see,' He gave the thread a tug, then wound it towards him, looping it around his index finger with delicate movements. 'Just as I thought,' he said. He held out the end of the thread to show Charlotte and her mother that it was empty. The doctor said the size and toxicity of the frog lodged in Charlotte's mother's throat could be altered with diet, but removal was preferable, which would require an operation.

'I'm not having an operation,' said Charlotte's mother. 'I'm nearly seventy, you know.'

'In fact, you're seventy-two,' the doctor said, glancing at his notes.

'Seventy-two,' cried Charlotte's mother. 'Exactly!'

'The procedure is fairly straightforward. You're not in any danger while the frog remains this size, but we don't want it growing any bigger.'

After the consultation, they stopped off at Hassan's.

'Got the list?' Charlotte's mother asked her, and Charlotte showed her the piece of notepaper on which she had written the items they needed. She had listed them in the order they would find them while travelling around the shop. Vegetables first, then refrigerated goods, then dry food and tins.

'How are you ladies?' Hassan asked, when they reached the till. 'Healthy, wealthy and wise?'

'Not so wealthy,' Charlotte's mother answered, heaving their wire shopping basket on to the counter. 'Nor healthy, neither—one or other of us has always got a cold or a sniffle.'

'I'm sorry to hear that,' Hassan said.

He opened a carton of Barn Fresh Eggs and tilted it towards Charlotte. She checked the eggs and nodded. He closed the box and slid it across the counter.

'Well, that's us done,' Charlotte's mother said, after their bags were packed and she had paid.

'That's you done, yes,' said Hassan.

'We'll be seeing you again.' She snapped her purse shut.

As they made their way back home, she complained that Hassan talked so much it was difficult to get a word in edge-ways.

Once they were indoors, Charlotte set the shopping bags on the kitchen floor and put the kettle on. While she was waiting for the water to boil, she knelt next to the shopping, contemplating tins and packets that had passed through Hassan's hands ('haath') and would pass through hers as she put them away.

Later, Charlotte sat on the sofa while her mother dozed in her chair in front of the news. She took the notepad her mother kept for working out crossword clues and wrote her name and Hassan's name over and over. A cooing sound, which she at first thought was inside her head, seemed to be coming from outside. She quickly peeled the page out of the notepad and tore it into tiny pieces, burying the fragments at the bottom of the wastepaper basket so her mother had no chance of finding them. Looking out of the window, she expected to see the pair of wood pigeons that sometimes came, but the lawn was empty. Stunted winter stalks showed through brown soil. She muted the television, and in the new quiet she discovered that the cooing sound was coming from inside the room. She checked behind the curtains and switched off all the plugs, before realising the noise was coming from her mother. She fetched a torch from the meter cupboard and shone it into her mother's mouth, like the handsome doctor had done, but the cooing stopped and the beam of the torch was too weak to see anything beyond her mother's glistening tonsils. Afraid of what her mother might do if she woke up, Charlotte put the torch away and sat still for the rest of the afternoon, listening to the cooing.

The day of the operation arrived.

'Wakey-wakey,' Charlotte whispered, creeping in to her mother's bedroom in the early morning.

'Why are you speaking like that?' her mother asked.

'I'm talking to the frog,' Charlotte said. 'I think it's beginning to recognise me.'

They walked to the bus stop, Charlotte carrying the small overnight bag she had packed for her mother. The streets were empty and Hassan was only just opening up his shop. Charlotte gave him a wave and he waved back.

'As next of kin, you'll need to give us your contact details,' the doctor told her when they arrived.

He handed her a pen from the pocket of his shirt. Today's shirt was a delicate shade of lavender. The pen was warm from his body. She filled out the form he gave her.

'The nurse will give you a call when the operation is complete,' he told Charlotte, smiling. 'Now take some time off — go into town and do a bit of shopping, or have a coffee — whatever it is that you ladies get up to.'

Charlotte watched her mother get wheeled away down the hospital corridor before she turned around and walked out of the building. She called in to see Hassan on her way home, but Noor was behind the till instead. She was wearing a red tunic, and loose cotton trousers to match. The material of her outfit was flecked with gold.

'Where's Hassan?' Charlotte asked.

Noor indicated with a nod of her head that he was in the stock room, separated from the shop by a ribboned doorway. The ribbons were greasy to the touch when Charlotte parted them. Hassan was sitting on a crate, surrounded by flattened cardboard boxes.

'Piyaalaa,' Charlotte said, pointing at the mug he held in his hand.

'Very good,' he said. He reached for a spoon and lifted it in the air.

'Chamcha.'

'Excellent. You're a fast learner, Charlotte.'

She stepped further into the dimly lit stockroom. 'What's the word for man?' she asked.

Soon it was time for her to go back to the hospital. Her mother's surgery had been successful, she was told, but her mother was a little depleted and they would like to keep her in for a few days.

When Charlotte arrived, the doctor was there to greet her, wearing green hospital scrubs, his dark hair flattened under a hairnet.

'How is it?' she asked.

'Your mother's fine,' he said, raising an eyebrow.

'What about the frog?'

'Ha! The frog, she says!' When he laughed, the skin around his eyes crinkled.

Charlotte asked him if she could see it and he led the way down shiny hospital corridors, walking with such long strides that she had to run to keep up. In a side room, the frog sat trembling in a tank. Charlotte and the doctor stood side by side looking at it.

'It's a fairly unusual condition,' he said. 'But not as uncommon as one might think. I've seen a few in my time.'

The frog gazed back at them.

'Can I keep it?' Charlotte asked, and the doctor said she could.

She found her way to the ward where her mother lay with her throat bandaged. She was too sore to talk, and too tired to communicate with anything more than an impatient flick of her hand, so Charlotte only stayed for a short while. Before leaving the hospital, she went to collect the frog. A plastic container was found and she rode home on the bus with it on her lap.

Hassan was stacking cardboard outside his shop. Charlotte told him her mother's operation had been a success.

'That's good news,' Hassan said.

'I've got something to show you,' Charlotte said, following him inside the shop. 'Can we go in there?' She gestured to the stockroom.

'Noor's at the cash and carry—I must stay behind the till,' Hassan said.

'It won't take long,' Charlotte said.

'There was a raid last week,' Hassan said. 'At the post office on Boundary Road.'

'Yes, I heard.'

'You read it in the paper?'

'Yes.'

'Do you want to buy a paper?'

'No, thank you.'

'Peppermints for your mother?'

'She's on liquids only for a while, so no.'

Hassan didn't want to see what Charlotte had to show him, so she took the frog home. In the bathroom, she ran a basin of water and tilted the container gently until the frog plopped into the sink and swam round and round in circles.

'Hungry, Frog?' she asked, when it stopped swimming, and the look on its sullen little face told her that it was. She fetched some lettuce and tore it into tiny shreds, which she scattered on the surface of the water. The frog snapped them up. She held out her palm and he jumped into her hand. In the kitchen, he sat patiently on the edge of the breadboard while she made herself a sandwich, and later, he seemed quite interested in the episode of Countdown he watched from the arm of her mother's chair.

Charlotte's mother's recovery took longer than anticipated. Days turned into weeks and weeks turned into months, but the period Charlotte spent at home, while her mother recuperated in hospital, was the happiest time of her life. She ate meals at odd hours and stayed up late into the night. She lived according to the frog's rhythms, and her own. She went to the library and borrowed books about amphibious life. The frog grew, and with money her mother had put aside for housekeeping, Charlotte bought him a lead, meant for a kitten or a miniature dog. He seemed to enjoy going for a walk on the leash. When it was raining, he would rest at the end of his tether, spreading his belly and his back legs flat, soaking up moisture from the pavement. Surprised neighbours would hail him from under their umbrellas, or call out to him over the tops of their dripping hedges, 'Morning, Froggy!' On sunny days, he wore a bonnet Charlotte took from one of her mother's dolls. It suited him very well.

One morning the telephone rang. Frog hopped in nervous circles on the hallway table.

'Charlotte,' her mother rasped, 'where are you? I'm sat here waiting!'

Charlotte told her mother she would be with her as soon as she could.

'I've been waiting for hours,' her mother complained, when Charlotte arrived at the hospital. 'The nurse said you'd be here in a tick. "She'll be here in a tick," she said—it's all she kept saying. Where were you?'

'I'm here now, Mother—let's get you home,' Charlotte replied.

They caught a bus and alighted outside Hassan's shop.

'Do we need anything?' her mother asked.

'No,' Charlotte said. 'I've got everything.'

'I'd like a nice cup of tea,' her mother said, as soon as they were indoors, 'not the dishwater they bring you in hospital. Make me a proper cup, will you?'

Charlotte filled the kettle, while her mother went into the bathroom. She was getting two mugs out of the cupboard when a loud shriek made her drop them, breaking one of the handles off. She ran into the bathroom where her mother stood with one hand clutching her throat. Frog was sitting in the sink where she had left him.

'Oh, you found Frog,' Charlotte said. 'Frog, this is Mother. Mother, Frog. But of course, you two know each other already.'

'You can't keep a disgusting thing like that in the house!' her mother yelled.

'Don't talk like that,' Charlotte said. 'He understands everything you say.'

Frog blinked at them from between the taps.

'It's revolting! Get rid of it,' her mother said.

They stood at each end of the bathroom mat staring at one another.

'If Frog goes, I go,' Charlotte said, and there was a different tone in her voice when she said it. Charlotte heard it, and her mother heard it too.

The Mermaid and the Tick

A HUSBAND AND WIFE lived by the sea. He was a handyman and she was a baker. Every day, after her baking was done, the wife would go down to the beach for a swim. In summer she lay on the shingle to dry off in the sun, and in winter she played chicken with the waves. Her husband joked that she was part mermaid, she loved the sea so much.

One day, the husband told his wife he had booked them a holiday. 'I thought it would be nice to go away before the baby comes,' he said. The ten-day holiday would be in Italy. The husband showed the wife a map of where they were going.

'It's quite far from the sea,' the wife said.

'There's a pool where we're staying,' he told her. The husband didn't like the beach. The pebbles hurt his feet and he had never learned to swim. He preferred the land, spending his weekdays mowing lawns and laying tiles, driving from job to job in a van with his name and telephone number written on the side. He showed his wife photographs of the holiday accommodation he had booked. There were cottages on the edge of a forest. Walking and cycling were recommended.

The wife bought a new, red swimming costume and ordered euros from the local bank. The husband booked a rental car, which they would pick up at the airport. On the plane, the wife did her knitting and the husband listened to music. Theirs was a late flight and it was night when they landed. The air was warm and sweet when they stepped off the plane.

'We're on holiday!' the wife said, and she gave a little hop and a skip as they crossed the tarmac in the perfumed darkness to where their hire car was waiting for them.

The husband drove and the wife was his navigator. The illuminated screen of her phone lit up her face as she followed directions and spoke them out loud. Soon, they turned off the main road from the airport and drove into a forest. A signpost with the travel company's name on it told them they had arrived. The car's headlights revealed low buildings arranged in a horseshoe shape around a small, oval swimming pool. The husband switched off the engine and they got out of the car. The night air was soft and warm and noisy with the sounds of crickets and frogs.

The key was in the door of their cottage and they let themselves in. There was an oven, a sink, and a table and two chairs. The linoleum was brown and the walls were white. They opened the back door to allow some air in. Light spilled out from the porch and into the dark expanse of the forest beyond.

In the bedroom, two orange towels lay folded on the bed. It was late and they were tired and hungry from their journey so they decided to go to sleep. The wife undressed, but when she went to lay her head on the pillow, she noticed spots of blood on the sheets.

'Mosquitoes,' her husband said.

He had read about insects in the area and had packed a special candle in his suitcase. He lit it now, and told his wife to lift her hair out of the way so he could rub insect repellent on to her neck and shoulders. He sprayed his own neck and arms while the wife looked for clean bedlinen in the cupboards, but there was none. They stripped the bed and lay on the orange towels.

In the morning, they were woken early by sounds of children playing. Loud splashes and squawks came from the swimming pool in front of the cottage. They pulled aside the curtains and watched a family who were staying in one of the neighbouring cottages. There was a father, a mother, and three children. Their cottage door was open and clothes hung on a washing line. The husband and wife watched the mother dry her child by the edge of the pool. The child stood with his arms out, like Christ on the cross. His tiny penis waggled as his mother briskly rubbed his body with an orange towel.

They were hungry, but they had no food. They would have to drive to the nearest town. In daylight, the husband saw that he had parked their hire car under a fig tree. Fruit had fallen during the night and lay splattered on the bonnet of the car. His wife came out of the cottage and locked the door, pocketing the key. She waved to the mother who had been drying her child, and the other woman waved back. When the wife saw the car, she glanced up into the laden branches of the tree and said she would make a pie with the figs.

They drove to a village, where they bought bread and milk

and eggs from the only shop. The shop's owner was a small, unsmiling woman.

'What's Italian for flour?' the wife asked her husband, but her husband didn't know. He googled it on his phone, but the shopkeeper shook her head.

Back at the holiday cottage, the husband cooked eggs for breakfast, while the wife stood in the doorway of their cottage, one hand resting on the top of her stomach.

'They've got three children,' she told the husband. She watched as the other family loaded up their car and drove away. 'Do you think they've left?' the wife asked.

'Probably just an outing,' her husband said.

Sunlight shone through the thin cotton of her dress and he could see the contours of her body against the bright doorway.

After they had eaten, the wife changed into her new red swimming costume and slipped into the pool. Her husband sat on the side with his feet hanging in the water. He watched his wife swim around and around.

'I could teach you, if you like,' she offered, flipping on to her back. The swell of her belly broke the surface of the water.

'I don't want to learn,' her husband said. 'I just like watching you.'

He went inside the villa, leaving wet footprints on the linoleum floor.

The other family returned, unloading bags of shopping from their car. The husband watched out of the window as his wife waved to them from her plastic sun lounger. Her red swimming costume hung from a branch of the tree. She held one hand up to her eyes, shielding them from the glare of the sun, as she spoke to the other woman. The children ran inside their cottage, then moments later, ran out again in their bathing suits. They leaped into the water, hugging their knees to their chests. Their mother yelled at them, and his wife laughed. Her wet hair clung to her shoulders.

'There's a big supermarket,' she told him, when she came indoors. 'We need to take the right-hand turn at the fork in the road. We took the wrong turning.'

They took a walk into the forest. Sunlight striped through the trees. In a clearing they found a shed. They tested the door, but it was locked. When they looked through the window, they could see neatly piled logs and an axe.

The next day, they drove to the supermarket. They passed through a village with a church and a pizzeria.

'Looks nice,' the husband said.

'We go straight on from here,' his wife said, so he carried on driving.

The supermarket was vast and brightly lit. It glittered like a palace and its aisles were packed with food of every description—fresh fruit and vegetables, newly baked loaves and pastries, boxes of unfamiliar breakfast cereals, an array of wine, chocolates and beers.

'Sheets!' the wife exclaimed, holding up a square of neatly packed bedlinen.

They treated themselves to luxuries they wouldn't afford themselves at home, including the bedsheets. When they returned, two new cars were parked outside the cottages, their bonnets pointed towards one another. Men were sitting on chairs on the scrubby grass beside the pool, drinking beers and cracking nuts, while the women were playing cards on a cottage patio, in the shade. The children were diving for something on the floor of the pool, chattering to one another in a language the husband and wife didn't recognise.

The husband and wife got out of their car and unloaded their shopping. The wife unhooked her red swimming costume from the tree and brought it inside the cottage.

'Why don't we go over and say hello?' she said.

'I prefer it when it's just you and me,' said the husband.

They replaced the bed linen, unfolding the new sheets between them, allowing them to billow up above the bed in their hands and fall softly down.

He asked if she wanted to go for another walk in the forest.

'I think I'll stay here,' she said, dragging a wooden chair into the doorway of the cottage. She settled herself in the chair with her knitting.

The forest was fragrant and full of shadows. He filled his lungs with its dry scented air and walked in the cool, dark silence, listening to the splinter of pine needles under his feet. When he came across the little shed, he walked around it and found an old wheelbarrow. He took its handles and flakes of rust came off in his hands. He wheeled the wheelbarrow back through the trees until he came to their cottage. He parked it next to the back door.

His wife wasn't inside the cottage and she wasn't sitting in her chair in the cottage doorway. He didn't know where she was—until he looked across to where the other families were. She was sitting among them, her knitting on her lap. She was laughing and chatting with a woman, while the children played in the pool. Another woman moved about, hanging up clothes and bathing suits to dry, gathering shoes, sun cream, inflatables and other toys that lay strewn around.

The husband took a beer from the fridge.

'This is the life,' he said to no one.

He held the bottle against his face, cooling his cheek and his forehead with the glass. He walked over to the cottage where his wife and the other women sat.

'Ah!' his wife said. 'My husband—mio marito.'

The husband held up his beer bottle and one of the women smiled and nodded. He tapped the top of the bottle and said, 'Open? Can you open it?'

The woman disappeared inside her cottage.

'I couldn't find an opener,' the husband told his wife.

'Not in a drawer in the kitchen?'

'I couldn't find one.'

The woman came out holding a bunch of keys. She handed them to the husband, showing him the bottle opener.

'Thank you,' the husband said, and the woman waved a hand, as if to say, 'It was nothing'.

The husband opened the bottle of beer and raised it in a toast. The woman answered him by raising the bottle of sun cream she held. He gave her back the keys.

On the third day, the husband woke up in an empty bed. He lay listening to the neighbours' children for a while and wondering where his wife was. He called out her name. When he looked out of the window, he saw her standing in the shallow end of the pool in her red swimming costume. The children swam around her, kicking their feet and splashing as they disappeared under the water then resurfaced, gasping, with their hair plastered over their eyes. They held out their arms to his wife and she took something from them, then raised her arm above her head and threw whatever it was. The children shrieked and bounded after it in a splashing mess, racing one another. When his wife lifted her arm, water streamed off her body in the sunlight. Her hair stuck to her shoulders like a cape of seaweed. One of the men lay on an orange towel next to the pool, pretending to be asleep.

'Looks like you're having fun,' the husband said loudly, coming to stand in the cottage doorway.

'They're diving for treasure,' his wife called back.

He walked to the edge of the pool. The gold coin his wife had thrown glinted on the bottom.

Later that day, his wife took a nap and he walked into the forest once more. This time, he ran his fingers over the shingled wood of the little shed, and feeling around, he found a key hanging on a hook underneath the windowsill. He tried it in the lock and the door of the shed opened with no difficulty at all.

Inside, the smell of the forest was even more pungent. Once his eyes had adjusted to the gloom, the husband lifted the small axe off its hook and went to find a tree to chop. When he found a tree he felt capable of cutting, he planted his feet wide and swung the axe, bringing it across his body. The axe bit into the flesh of the tree with such force he grunted like an animal. He crouched down to study the gash he had made, stroking the tree's creamy insides.

He was thirsty when he arrived back at the cottage. A fig pie sat on the kitchen counter, halved fruits studding the pastry, like jewels. It was warm to his touch. Ants were feasting on a saucepan sticky with honey, and a bowl and a spoon stood in the sink. He filled a glass with water and drank it down. Filling his glass once more, he took a sip then poured the rest into the mixing bowl, causing it to overflow. He stood still, feeling his pulse beating in his neck, watching the milky-coloured water gurgle down the plughole.

'Come and see how much wood I've cut,' he said to his wife.

She was sitting outside the front of the cottage. Her hair was damp and she was evening out the wool on her knitting needles, counting her stitches. She rested the lemon-yellow blanket she was knitting on the bump of her belly.

'Come and see how much wood I've cut,' he said, once more.

His wife put away her knitting and he led the way into the forest, wheeling the rusty wheelbarrow. In the shed they stood side by side, staring at the pile of logs he had chopped.

'You're a proper lumberjack,' she told him, and they made love on the warm forest floor.

Halfway through the holiday, he began to itch in bed at night. His wife complained that he was keeping her awake with his scratching. An angry red rash appeared on his waist, so they drove to the little town once more, and went to see a doctor.

The doctor was a small, neat man, who seemed to understand what they were saying, even though he didn't speak English. He gestured for the husband to take off his shirt and walked around him, running his fingers over his belly and back.

'*Stato nella foresta?*'

The husband could tell the doctor was asking a question because of the way his voice went up at the end of his sentence. '*Non parlo…*' he said.

'The house where we're staying is next to a forest,' his wife told the doctor, and the doctor nodded, moving behind his desk where he tapped something on the keyboard of a computer. He turned the screen round so they could read it.

'Tick,' said the wife. 'He thinks you've been bitten by a tick.'

They watched the doctor cross the room to fetch a pair of tweezers from a metal pot. He signalled to the husband to lift his arms, and the husband closed his eyes while the doctor inspected him, carefully parting his armpit hair with the tweezers. The doctor took a step backwards and gestured for the husband to drop his shorts. The man glanced at his wife before doing as he was asked. The doctor pointed at his underwear, and he pulled down his boxers, tipping his head back to stare at the ceiling.

Bending to examine his groin, the doctor made a noise and beckoned to the wife to look at her husband's skin.

'I can see it!' she exclaimed.

The husband closed his eyes while his wife and the doctor bent close to his body. He listened to a rattle of speech coming from the doctor.

'Can you just ask him to get it out, please?' he said.

'Have you got a signal?' his wife asked. 'Ask Siri what 'gonfio' means.'

'Just ask him to get it out,' the husband repeated.

As he spoke, he felt a pressure against his skin, and with a deft movement of his tweezers the doctor extracted the creature.

'That's it?' the husband asked.

'That's it,' the doctor replied, in English. 'You are free to go.'

The midday sun shone fiercely, reflecting off the pale gravel of the town square and the white walls of the surrounding buildings.

'Shall we look inside the church?' the woman asked, squinting.

'Later.'

They headed across the square to a restaurant. The tables outside were busy, but a couple were leaving—the woman gathered up her jacket, while the man tossed a few coins into a white saucer. He smiled at the husband and wife as they took their place. A waiter cleared away the glasses and pocketed the coins.

'What are you going to have?' the wife asked, studying the menu.

'Pizza, maybe,' the husband replied. 'When in Rome.'

His wife said she would have spaghetti alle vongole. She wanted to wash her hands before they ate and asked her husband to order for her. While she was gone, the husband googled *tick bite* on his phone.

'That doctor should have given me a blood test,' he said, when she came back to the table. He passed her his phone to show her the page he had been reading.

She squinted at the tiny writing on the screen. 'Any flu like symptoms?' she asked.

'No.'

'Any chest pain?'

He shook his head.

'I'm sure you'll be fine.'

The waiter came and took their order and then they lapsed into silence while they waited for their food to arrive. On the other side of the piazza, a couple were unpacking their car. The man of the couple opened the boot and pulled out a pushchair, while the woman reached inside the car and lifted out a child. They strapped the child into the pushchair, locked their car, and walked away, disappearing down one of the side streets next to the church. The husband stared at the pale stone church, its walls carved with gargoyles. Horned demons scowled at sinners below.

'Alright?' the wife asked. She reached across the table to place her hand on her husband's.

'I'd quite like to go,' he said.

'But we just ordered.'

'Home,' her husband said. 'I'd like to go home.'
She removed her hand, resting it on top of her stomach.
'Soon,' she replied.

An Extra Teat

THE WHOLE FAMILY wakes up in one bed, clinging to its sides like shipwrecked sailors. After much sniffing and sighing, Doug rolls over and crashes on to the floor, landing on all fours. 'For fuck's sake!'

First words of the day.

He yanks his dressing gown off the back of the bedroom door. Kit is lying on Caro's hair, so she can only lift her head minutely to watch her husband as he stumbles out of the room.

'Is it school today?' Josie asks on waking.

First words of the day.

She came into their room in the night again and has slept curled up at the bottom of the bed.

'Is it school today?' she asks again.

It isn't clear to Caro whether she wants it to be a school day or not.

'School, and then Granny's, while Mummy's at work,' she tells her daughter.

She eases her hair out from underneath Kit's sleeping body and sits up, reaching for a hairband to tie her dreadlocks back. Nine months old, Kit was feeding most of the night—or, at least, that's what it felt like. Caro presses both hands to her breasts—they feel full again, already. She squeezes some nipple cream out of a tube, massages it in.

'I need some!' Josie says, bouncing on her knees in front of Caro. Her movement on the bed jiggles Kit, who heaves a shuddering sigh.

'Don't wake him up.'

'Booby cream!' Josie hoists up her nightie, baring her skinny little body.

Caro dabs a spot of cream on to each of her little girl's nipples.

'Is a snog the same as a long kiss?' she asks her mother.

'Yes, I suppose so,' Caro says. 'Who's been talking about snogs?'

Jo-Jo doesn't answer, but leaps off the bed and runs out of the room.

Downstairs, the coffee machine growls.

'Did you make me one?' Caro asks.

'You were asleep.'

'Not since four.'

Doug grunts.

She puts Kit in his highchair, calls to Josie to come to the table and eat her cereal.

'I think Jo-Jo's coming into bed with us because she knows Kit's in there. She feels left out.'

'And remind me, why is Kit in with us?'

'It's his teeth.'

Doug lays his phone face down on the table. 'It's always his teeth. And if it's not his teeth, it's his arse. And if it's not Kit's arse, it's Jo-Jo's.'

His phone pings, but he ignores it. Caro doesn't recognise the sound of the notification—is he on Tinder? She tries to think if he was scrolling left or right when she came into the room, but she's so tired she can barely remember her own name. She cuts up an apple like an automaton, handing the pieces to Kit before remembering they were for Josie's lunchbox.

Once they are dressed and getting ready to leave, Doug starts up about the house being a mess. Whenever he is stressed, the piles of washing everywhere, the scattered toys, the sticky furniture all become suddenly intolerable.

'Can't you do something about this bath?' he snarls, as she crouches over Kit on the changing mat on the floor.

'Do what about it?'

'Clean it, for once? Do something about all the fucking wildlife in here?' He's scooping out handfuls of plastic animals and bath toys.

'Teeth, Jo-Jo,' Caro says.

She could point out that Doug is lucky to be thinking about having a bath, when she is wrestling Kit into a clean nappy, getting Josie ready for school, and herself ready for her day's work, but she says nothing. He's always like this when he's got a deadline.

She stares at him as he bends over the bath, sloshing water violently around the tidemark.

. . .

Caro wheels her bike up to the school. Her cardigan has hung on the chair overnight and its wool has puckered into a kind of third teat. She tugs at it, trying to re-shape it, while steering her bike and keeping it from tipping over with Kit on the back.

On the journey, Josie won't stop talking.

'Mummy, what would happen if I ate myself?' she asks.

'Pay attention now, wait for the green person.'

Josie presses the button and feels underneath for the touch signal for the partially sighted. While they wait for the lights to change, she repeats her question.

'If I ate myself, would I be fat, or would I disappear?' She looks up at her mother, waiting for an answer. 'Mum-my! Are you listening to me?'

'I am listening, Jo-Jo, but I'm going to have to think about that one,' Caro says.

They cross the road and she points out the dog shit on the other side that she doesn't want Josie to step in.

'Mummy, what if a Diplodocus laid down, then what?'

'Mmm?'

'Would it still be as big as a house?'

The only pause in her child's chatter comes when they pass the estate agent's, where every morning they see a homeless person lying in the doorway, humped in a blue sleeping bag that covers their face. Once they have moved past, Josie asks Caro in a whisper why that person doesn't live with their mum and dad.

'Perhaps he doesn't like them,' Caro suggests.

'Were they mean to him?' her daughter asks.

In the school playground, Caro waits for the bell to ring while Josie and her friends run around her bike, tugging at Kit, pulling off his hat and chucking it to one another, making him cackle. When the teachers come into the playground, she watches her child line up with the rest of her class. Josie files inside the school building without a backward glance. Caro straightens Kit in his seat on the back of the bike, then says goodbye to the other mothers and cycles on to her parents' house.

'Here she is, the Working Mum!' Caro's mother flings open the front door and holds out her arms for Kit. She asks Caro if she's got time to come up to the spare bedroom. She wants to show her the colour she plans to paint it. She plonks Kit on Caro's father's knee, and Kit bounces up and down, expecting 'This is the Way the Gentlemen Ride'.

'We're thinking of Plantation Green,' her mother informs her, standing in the middle of the room that used to be Caro's own. 'And I'll do the woodwork in cream. What do you think?' She holds out the paint colour chart for Caro's approval and the charms on her bracelet rattle. 'I always fancied myself as something of an interior decorator.'

'You can't paint it Plantation Green, Mum,' Caro says.

'I knew you'd say that,' her mother says, throwing down the colour chart and stalking out of the room.

'You better tek him,' her father says, when they go back downstairs, wincing slightly as he hands Kit back, then he stares vacantly into space, fingering the pile of junk mail sitting on the leather pouffe next to his chair.

Caro takes Kit through to the kitchen, where her mother has begun washing up the breakfast things.

'Dad seems low.'

'Ssh, I'm listening.' Lauren Laverne is talking to a military commander about the musical instruments he played as a child.

'He is low,' her mother whispers. 'I can't do a thing with him.'

She shuttles her charm bracelet up her arm and plunges both hands into the sink. Caro sits Kit on the floor—he can hold himself upright now. She finds a cork for him to play with, rattles it back and forth inside an empty margarine tub she gets off the draining board. She tips the cork out to show him, and puts it back in the tub again, rattling it back and forth. Lauren Laverne's conversation with the military commander gives way to a strident orchestral piece.

'Oh, dear Lord, that's horrible,' her mother says, wiping her hands and slamming the volume down. 'Who wants that racket on a desert island?' She tuts at the blob of washing up foam on her radio. Then asks Caro, 'What would you choose, for your luxury?'

'I don't know. I've never thought about it.'

'Well, think about it now. Come on!'

Caro studies her mother for a moment. Soapsuds cling to the charm bracelet, which she's worn since Caro was a child. She's wearing a pair of gold sandals and a printed smock.

'A fork, maybe? To work the land.' She really needs to leave, so she can get to her client on time.

Her mother turns her head to stare at her, her hands still resting under the bubbles in the sink. Caro can name each individual charm on her bracelet.

Bottle of rum.

'And that's what you'd ask for, is it? A gardening fork?'

'Yes.'

Spanish guitar.

'Well that's a very boring choice, if I may say so, Caroline. A very boring choice.' She seems angry, but Caro doesn't know why.

On the floor between them, Kit rattles the cork in the margarine tub and smacks the patterned floor tiles with his fat little hands.

Feather.

Mouse.

'What would yours be then?'

'Well, something luxurious for a start! Some kind of treat. Nothing of any *use*, that's the point.'

Tramp's boot.

Painter's palette.

'Gardening tools would feel like a luxury to me. They're beautiful objects, I think, and full of what's possible.'

'"Full of what's possible." Listen to you!'

The charms on her mother's bracelet flick and flack against one another as she dries her hands briskly on a tea towel.

Leprechaun.

'I suppose I could make a fork, couldn't I?' Caro says. 'Whittle a branch and sharpen the prongs with a stone, or whatever. Tie it together with bits of vine.'

'Sweet Jesus!'

Her mother scoops Kit off the floor, slams the margarine tub back on to the draining board. The cork tumbles into the sink of frothy water.

'What's the matter?' Caro asks, looking at her mother.

They stand facing one another, Kit in between them.

'Nothing's the matter.'

'You seem annoyed.' Caro reaches towards her baby, picking a bit of porridge out of his hair.

'Me? I'm not annoyed. You wouldn't be allowed garden tools, anyway,' her mother says as she leads the way back into the living room with Kit balanced on her hip. 'Anything to help you escape isn't allowed. Dig your way out with a gardening fork, easy.'

From her parents' house, Caro cycles on to her client, the baby seat bumping along emptily behind her. Richard is an elderly gentleman with one leg. Caro doesn't know what happened to his other leg—in spite of their lengthy and often intimate conversations, he has never mentioned it, as if he would prefer not to think about it. Caro has worked for him since Josie was small.

'Good morning, fair maiden,' he calls, when she wheels her bike around the side of the house. He's already waiting for her on the gravel path.

'Hello,' she says.

'And how are we today?'

'Fine.'

'Oh dear,' he says. 'Come and tell Dickie all about it.'

He reverses his wheelchair so she can get past him and she leads the way to her potting shed, where she makes them both a cup of tea. The shed is furnished with a tatty armchair, where she can sit when it's raining, and a desk, where she keeps her damp-mottled gardening books and seed catalogues. Crowded with lopsided towers of germinating trays and plant pots, the space is too small for Richard's wheelchair, so he parks in the doorway and she passes him his mug. Wintry sunlight shines on his bald, pink head.

He asks after Doug and the children, and quizzes her on what she thinks about the latest government fiasco. Politically, they view the world differently, but this doesn't stop him listening to her reasons for thinking the way she does, and this came as a surprise for Caro.

When they have finished their tea, he hands her his empty

mug and they make a tour of the garden, with Richard pointing out this or that plant, asking her what she recommends for this or that spot, what would suit the soil and light and weather conditions. They designed the garden together, and his budget is seemingly boundless. Caro knows he worked in the city and inherited family money as a young man.

The garden is divided into four quarters, each representing a different period of his life. Nearest the house—visible only through a gap in the laurel bushes Caro would prefer to cut down—is a planted section representing his childhood in India. Jasmine and a climbing rose grow up the side wall, and there's a small water garden where they have had some success with lotus flowers. Copper and gold marigolds are flowering in one bed, next to another planted with dahlias. Richard's preference was for yellow and apricot varieties, but she persuaded him to introduce some crimsons and dark reds, and he enjoyed her joke when she told him she had ordered one called 'Be A Sport'.

Next to the childhood beds, separated by a gravel path wide enough for his wheelchair, is a section commemorating Richard's professional life, with honesty among the planting, and gold and yellow flowers, including hollyhocks, yellow roses, and rows of ornamental cabbage.

The third quarter signifies his marriage and family life. His wife is dead, but remembered in an 'Annabel' rose that does very well, and in a hybrid tea rose, 'Ruby Celebration'. Caro has met his grown-up children. She will never forget the look of disgust that flickered across his daughter's face when he introduced Caro as his right-hand woman. It was an awkward moment.

The section of garden dedicated to Richard's old age is the section they continue to discuss as a 'work in progress'. Caro suggested making it a meadow and allowing it to grow a little wild, seeing what Nature will bring to their design—an idea that appealed to the old man. They have sown wild flowers, including poppies and daisies, which are the names of his grandchildren, but the rest they have left to chance. His family have criticised this section of the garden, though, telling him it looks scruffy and out of keeping with the rest. He passes on their criticism, but assures her he doesn't expect her to do anything about it. He is happy with her work.

He asks her if they should call in a tree surgeon to deal with a cypress pine, whose branches are casting part of the garden in shade.

'I'd prefer not to,' Caro says.

'Leave it to Mother Nature?' Richard asks her, in a gently mocking tone.

'Something like that,' she says, looking up into the tree's branches.

'I agree,' he says. 'Enough lopping and chopping and taking away.'

She can't be certain, but she thinks he gestures at his leg.

She spends the morning digging a new bed. It's hard, physical work. She drapes her cardigan over a low wall, and while she turns over the earth with her spade, she thinks about what Josie will be doing at school. She might be drawing or making something out of cereal boxes, or tracing around numbers with arrows to show which way her pen should travel. When Caro's at work, she thinks about her children, and when she's with her children, she dreams about work. She tries to concentrate on the brown earth under her spade. An earthworm writhes and she flings it aside.

Towards lunchtime, she hears Kit's familiar cry at the side gate. He is beginning to find his voice. Richard allows her a flexible working arrangement—when she breaks for lunch, her mother brings Kit to her and she breastfeeds him before his afternoon nap. After a feed, he'll mostly sleep for an hour, or even for a good two hours in a travel cot in the corner of her potting shed while she works nearby. On the odd occasion that he only naps for twenty minutes, she brings him out to sit on the lawn while she finishes off her jobs, and Richard is fine with that.

'Here's his lordship,' her mother says, handing Caro the changing bag.

She picks up her child and her mother turns the empty buggy around and wheels it down the side of the house.

'We had a good morning,' she says, as she goes.

'Thanks, Mum,' Caro calls after her.

Her mother and her one-legged boss never meet, as if the two parts of Caro's life—the professional and personal—must be kept separate. She has the impression her mother disapproves of Richard for some reason—she purses her lips whenever Caro talks about him.

Caro takes Kit to the potting shed, walking him around its musty cobwebby walls, showing him the pictures in her seed catalogues. He arches in her arms, lurching away from her, away from the seed catalogues, rubbing his ear with his fat little fist. She puts her deformed cardigan back on and settles in the old armchair, breathing in its damp upholstery, laying a muslin square over its scratchy arm. She exposes one breast and feels Kit relax in her arms as he latches on. His eyes close, and his body slackens. She takes one of his podgy feet in her hand and her own body floods with relief as he begins to suck.

She closes her eyes and tips back her head. The only sound in the shed is the gentle pop of Kit's throat as he gulps. Caro wonders if Richard will come. He doesn't always. She is disappointed when he doesn't. A blackbird calls as it streaks across the lawn behind the shed. Somewhere in the distance, she can hear the beeping reverse signal of a delivery van. Then a crunch of gravel close by tells her he is near. She keeps her eyes closed, soft shafts of light filtering through her eyelids. The sun is still low this early in the year. Richard often wheels his chair to sit watching her as she feeds, but she never acknowledges him. They have an unspoken pact. Neither of them mentions the arrangement they have come to. She wonders if he is turned on by it. Horribly, she would like it if he was.

Mother and child and one-legged man remain in their positions until the regular pulse of Kit's suck slows. Then his body is suddenly alert, stiffening in her arms as he lets go of her nipple. She opens her eyes and he is staring up at her. Her breast is exposed, its milky brown-ness, darker than her mother's skin, lighter than her father's, is barely visible in the dusty light of the shed. She avoids his gaze, listens to the creak of his wheelchair as he moves out of view. Kit makes a sound, and when she looks down at her child, he is staring up at her.

'Are you trying to tell me something?' she asks him. 'Are you trying to tell me something, mister?'

Her baby finds her nipple once more, and she closes her eyes. Soon his body grows heavy in her lap. If she moves, he'll wake up again. She sits still, eyes closed. What will she cook this evening? Doug will complain if she cooks pasta again. She'll text him and ask him to pick up something paleo on his way back from work. He's a caveman, but he's always on his phone. She pictures Jo-Jo's lunchbox, which she will empty when she gets home—its sandwich crusts, browning apple pieces, and cheese wrapper. She looks forward to seeing what shape her daughter's fingers will have moulded the Babybel red wax into. For once, she would like to live in the moment. To live properly and wholly in any given moment, no part of her elsewhere. On a desert island, maybe.

The Painting

LOTTA'S HUSBAND, Vik, was good at presents, and this year he had excelled himself. This year, he had commissioned a painting for his wife's birthday. It would be a family portrait. Vik and Lotta both had curly hair—his dark, hers fair. Their children had curly hair too. They would make a wonderful composition, Vik thought, and when he showed the painter photos of them all on his phone, she agreed.

He had chosen a female artist, believing a woman would be sympathetic to the subject. Her name was Eve. Eve could paint from photographs, but she suggested some sittings would be helpful. These would take place in secret and would be easy to arrange, as Lotta commuted to London and often didn't arrive home until after the children's bedtime.

Eve arrived for the first sitting wearing her clothes inside out. The label of her green silk blouse fluttered at its seam. She had ink-stained hands, and her fingernails were blackened from charcoal. Her straight hair fell down her back like a cape. Vik noticed the way his daughter stared at her, bewitched by her jangling rings and necklaces, her belt buckle and curious bangles.

She asked the children how they wanted to pose, suggesting they might like to be painted holding a beloved toy, or an object. The boy, Jack, chose to stand wielding the longbow he had made at a mediaeval workshop the previous summer. India sat cross-legged on the floor, as she did at school, hands neatly clasped in her lap.

'And you,' Eve asked Vik, 'how would you like to pose?'

They discussed whether he should stand, or sit, or kneel next to his children. Eve smiled a lot when she spoke, and seemed to pant slightly. Vik found himself asking her questions—about her painting, about its composition and her technique—just so that she would keep talking in her charming, breathless way. He chose to sit in the wing-backed chair inherited from Lotta's parents.

'Wonderful,' Eve said, bobbing around, her jewellery tinkling, while he moved the chair into position. She narrowed her eyes, squinting at him, as he sat motionless, his hands resting on the arms of the chair.

'It gives us useful height,' she said.

He enjoyed the feel of her eyes on him, and the sound of the scratch of her brush. When she moved close, he could smell roses.

'What's Mummy going to wear in the painting?' India asked, fingering the lace trim of her Best Dress. 'Not her work clothes. She looks like a man.'

The Painting

In the early stages of the painting, as Eve identified each figure in patches of bold colour, her movements were swift. But over the weeks, as she closed in on them, refining their detail, she worked more slowly, and she would duck behind her canvas for longer periods before reappearing to squint at them once more. Jack was always the first to tire, so she would begin with his figure, and once she was satisfied, she had what she needed, she would send him off to play. Vik watched his daughter pluck at her tights, pulling the fabric away from her leg and watching it ping back, and he knew that she was as in love with Eve as he was.

'You've really captured something,' he told Eve one afternoon, when the painting was almost finished.

'Yes, I'm pleased with it,' she said.

They were standing next to one another staring at her work. She tucked her brush behind her ear and a thin ribbon of brilliant-green paint streaked her hair. Vik was afraid he would explode with desire.

'Paint...in your hair,' he croaked, reaching out to tease the offending strand. A smell of warm coconut reached his nostrils —her shampoo, perhaps. Panic rose in his chest. He needed to find a way to carry on seeing her once the painting was finished.

He turned his attention back to the portrait.

'My feet look a bit...funny,' he said.

'They're not finished yet.'

They both stared at the painting. It made him look handsome, with his manly features and curly hair. The chair he sat in was handsome, too, high-backed, with printed upholstery.

'They look a bit funny,' he said.

The expression on her face grew serious, so he added, 'Well, I suppose they are funny, aren't they!' and he held out a leg to demonstrate the comedy of his own body.

'The angle of them, though,' Eve said, frowning at her picture, 'it's not right.'

She dabbed at the man's feet in the painting. The tuft of her brush flared and flattened as she pressed it against the canvas. Softly, softly, he thought to himself. Slowly does it. Maybe he could book painting lessons for the children? Or as part of Lotta's birthday present, even? Anything, in order to keep Eve coming to the house, to keep her in his sights.

His wife's birthday was on a Saturday, which worked out nicely, he thought. She could have a lie-in and open presents in bed with her breakfast. No need for her to be rushing out of the house like she did on weekdays. He placed the painting ceremoniously at the foot of their bed the night before, draping it in a piece of velvet from India's dressing-up box.

'Oh, what's this?' Lotta propped herself up higher against the pillows, putting aside the work she had been doing. 'Presents already?'

Vik glanced at the bedside clock, noting that it was past midnight and therefore technically her birthday.

'You're not allowed to look until the morning,' he told her. 'The kids are so excited.'

That night, he dreamed about Eve.

'Wake up! Wake up, it's Mummy's birthday!'

As he turned over, he sensed the empty space in the bed beside him before he opened his eyes.

'Wake up, sleepy head,' Lotta said, setting down a tray laden with toast and coffee.

'I should be doing that,' he mumbled, his mouth thick with sleep.

'I was up anyway,' she said. 'I'm not sure the kids can hold out much longer.'

Now it was Vik's turn to bank up the pillows behind him and sit up in bed.

'Can I?' Jack bleated. 'Can I?'

At his mother's signal, the boy whipped off the velvet to reveal the painting. Lotta gasped.

'Oh!' she exclaimed.

Vik sank back into the bed, sleepily satisfied with the surprise he had pulled off. He really was excellent at presents.

The children danced around their mother, tugging at her arms, asking her if she liked it.

'I do. I really do,' she said.

They ran from the room and he watched her prop the painting against the wardrobe, sitting on the end of the bed to study it. Her shoulders tightened, as if she was trying to stop herself from crying. She really was moved, he thought, taking a cup of coffee from the breakfast tray, and it was no wonder—Eve had done a fantastic job, capturing the light and bounce of their daughter's hair, the intensity of their son's frown, and his own, well, his own manliness, there was no other word for it. He took a sip of coffee.

'Where am I?' his wife whispered, turning to face him.

Her morning eyelashes were pale without their mascara.

'Where am I?' she asked once more, her voice cracking.

He looked at his wife and he looked at the painting. The tang of the coffee gave him a sudden urge to run out of the room. He took another sip, hiding his face in the cup to give him thinking time.

Camel Toe

WITH THEIR MOTHER'S death, Carys and her sister have been orphaned. They are middle-aged, but that doesn't stop Carys feeling this status of theirs keenly. Their father died when they were young, so they have both been daughters to a mother only.

'Us next,' Sara told her, before their mother's body was even in the ground.

Upstairs, the shower is going and Carys can hear her sister's dog whining from inside the bathroom, wanting to be let out. Sara is staying in the house while they arrange the funeral, and 'put their mother's affairs in order', as the solicitor put it. Carys doesn't understand why she refused her invitation to stay with her, but she knows not to go there.

Her sister is two years older and two years ahead of her, in most things—married two years before Carys, and had her first child two years before Carys had Owen. Sara got divorced two years ago. Carys wonders what this could mean for her and Garth. The clatter of the letterbox makes her jump, and she looks up to see the postman turn away from the rippled glass of the front door, his distorted figure moving along the low wall to the next house. She hears him knock at the neighbour's door, then a conversation about a parcel. The walls are so thin, she can hear every word. Her mother's stick stands sentry in the corner. It was the sight of it, as she let herself into the house this morning, that made Carys catch her breath and sit on the bottom stair, where she remains, Sainsbury's bag on lap, staring at the patterns in the carpet worn bare by her mother's feet.

Her phone pings. She reaches for her bag, which lies on the hallway floor.

Got no socks

She closes her eyes and tips her head back. When she opens them again, she leaves her head tipped back, chin to the ceiling. The textured plaster reminds her of Mum's Christmas cake. If they manage to sell, new owners will smooth it over. They'll replace the draughty windows and the old-fashioned glass in the front door. She asked Sara if they could rent the place out, instead of selling, but Sara said it would be too much hassle, and besides, she needs the money. Monthly rent payments are money, Carys had said. She quite fancied being someone's landlady and she would make sure she was a nice one, not like the criminals Owen had to deal with when he was at uni. She had pointed out how handy an ongoing income would be. 'A lump sum would be handier,' Sara said.

Borrow some from Dad? Carys texts back. She scoops up the mail and heaves herself to standing. Among the condolence cards and an eye test reminder, there is an offer to clear her mother's gutters, and a mailout from the council listing fitness activities across the vale. There are several classes designed for the elderly. Mum was busy enough with her church, but she might have enjoyed 'Armchair Aerobics'. She would have liked the armchair bit, anyway. *Rediscover Netball* is listed under *Fit and Fabulous at Fifty*, illustrated with a picture of a stick lady throwing a ball, ponytail flying. Sessions are held in the playground belonging to the school Carys and Sara went to when they were girls.

The bathroom door bangs and the dog bounds down the stairs, thwacking her legs with his tail as he shoves past. Sara thumps slowly down after him.

'Oh, it's you,' she says. 'When did you get here?'

She doesn't wait for an answer, squeezing past Carys and heading into the kitchen. Her hair is wet from the shower. She'll have used all the water. Carys will have to wait for the immersion before she makes a start on the crockery. In the kitchen, dog biscuits rattle into the metal bowl Sara brought with her. Carys can hear the dog chomping. She taps another message to Owen: *Put a wash on.*

She dumps the mail on the table in the front room. The table will go—Sara has stuck a yellow Post-it note on it, as she has with most of their mother's furniture. Who will take their mother's stick? It has no Post-it attached, so the house-clearance guys will leave it alone. It will likely still be propped in the corner when they close the door of their mother's house for the last time.

'Do you want a coffee?' her sister asks, poking her head through the dining hatch.

Carys shakes her head, and Sara shuts the doors of the hatch. A few moments later, Carys hears her trudge up the stairs and into her bedroom. Carys waits until she hears the door click shut before she goes into the kitchen. The sound of Sara's bedroom door closing is a sound she remembers from their girlhood.

Carys spends the morning boxing up the crockery. Sara's dog follows her from room to room, as she moves between the kitchen and the small dining room. He is a brindle greyhound, rescued from the track. When Carys looks at him, he gazes at her with sad brown eyes. She doesn't speak to him, apart from telling him to stay when she lets herself out of the house, carrying the plates and cups and glassware around the corner to the church hall. Together with Sandy, who runs the village coffee mornings, she unpacks her mother's belongings. Sandy says she will gladly take the books Carys has gathered from the bookcase, too, so Carys takes the empty box back to the house and fills it with romantic novels and Anthony Hopkins biographies. There's also a series of books on *Faith and the Family*, and one called *Difficult Daughters*. Carys sits back on her heels when she comes across this one. She flicks through its pages, imagining her mother reading the words she's reading. She wonders which of them was the difficult one. Sara living in Cardiff made things easier, and being a son, Matt was excluded from any 'difficulty'. He was safely abroad, anyway, though he would now be winging his way back from Buenos Aires for the funeral. She shoves the book deep inside the box. Then she thinks about Sandy, in her neat gold jewellery, laying it on a trestle table along with the other books, and she takes it out of the box and drops it into the kitchen bin instead.

Each journey she makes, with each heavy box of books, she avoids passing the bus stop where Mum had her fall. Every time she returns to the house, the stupid dog is there to greet her. Sara hasn't put in an appearance all day, and there is silence from upstairs. Carys cleans the empty shelves and cupboards, and she cooks a shepherd's pie in her mother's chipped Pyrex dish, with potatoes, mince, carrots and onions brought from home. The dog continues to shadow her. She doesn't speak to him, and she hasn't touched him yet. While the potato topping browns, she sets the table. Every evening, they've been sitting down to eat properly, instead of standing like Carys does at home—forking food into her mouth at the kitchen counter, while she scrolls through her phone, waiting for Owen and Garth to get back from work.

Tidying envelopes and wastepaper off the table, she spots the fitness leaflet featuring the stick lady and her netball.

For players of all levels. Everyone welcome.

There's a session tonight, and the thought of another evening with her sister stretching ahead of her has Carys calling up the stairs, 'How do you fancy a game of netball?'

It's quiet. The dog stands next to her. He lets out a whine.

They just have time to change and walk down the lane, retracing the steps they took every day, until Sara told her she was walking to school with Beth Evans from now on and Carys wasn't allowed to join them.

She climbs the stairs. The dog bounds ahead of her, his tail whacking the spindles. She knocks on her sister's bedroom door, but there's no answer, and when she pushes it open, the room is empty. Sara's suitcase lies open on the floor. One half contains neatly folded clothes packed into a zipped mesh compartment, while the other half spews pairs of trousers and socks, underwear and pyjamas, its contents strewn all around. Carys shuts the door and pads along the landing to their mother's room. She finds Sara sitting on a low velveteen stool at the dressing table, a flat, white box on her lap. She is surrounded by plump bin-bags and the wardrobe doors hang open, revealing empty hangers. The dog weaves around the room sniffing in corners, poking his snout into open drawers. He nudges the lid off the tatty white box on Sara's lap, and when Sara scolds him, he lays down next to her, his chin on his paws.

'There's a netball session for fabulous fifty-year-olds up at the school. You up for it?'

'Fabulous fifty-year-olds?'

'That's us.'

The two women look at each other, marooned among their mother's clutter. Carys can tell her sister has been crying.

'I haven't played netball in years,' Sara says.

'Nor me.'

'What'll we wear?'

'You've got daps, no?'

Sara shuffles around on the faded velveteen stool and sticks out one leg with a fat trainer on the end. She's wearing black leggings and a drapey printed top she thinks disguises the size of her bosom.

'Go as you are,' Carys says.

'You think?'

'I reckon so.'

'Two secs, while I change my bra.'

While she's out of the room, Carys looks inside the white box. It contains their mother's wedding dress and veil, neatly folded. She holds the box out for the dog to sniff, then she replaces the lid and sits on the bed. A yellow Post-it is stuck to the headboard. The bin-bags dotted around the place are stuffed with her mother's clothes. Once upon a time, the three of them were of a size, but Carys and Sara grew while Mum shrank. When she first met Garth, he commented, 'She's a bit of a dragon, your mum, isn't she?' but she was depleted by the end of her life, scaly and breathless. Carys riffles through the clothes her sister has sorted and finds a pair of beige nylon trousers. With an elasticated waist they are tracksuit bottoms by any other name, right? They'll be more comfortable to play netball in than her own clothes.

She eases off her jeans and pulls on her mother's trousers.

'Camel toe,' Sara says, coming into the room, as Carys stands to survey her reflection in the wardrobe mirror.

'You can talk,' Carys says, eyeing her sister, who has swapped her drapey top for a zip-up fleece. The seam of her leggings divides her in two.

Sara laughs, prodding her pudendum. 'Who knew it was possible to put on weight there, as well as everywhere else?'

They stand side by side, looking at themselves in their mother's mirror.

'I'm bald as a coot down there, are you?' Sara says.

'Better than the opposite,' Carys replies, and they both know the other is remembering young Miles Jefcoate following them home from school, singing lewd songs at them.

'What will you do with…?' Carys asks, nodding at the dog.

Sara assures her Billy will be no trouble, she won't even have to tie him up, he's that well behaved.

They leave the house by the back door, just like they used to, and press their bodies through the back gate, one by one. They used to fit through the gate more easily. Carys can taste the chill of early mornings and drifting mist, she can feel the stiffness of new leather shoes. Blackberries still grow in the scruffy brambles along the back wall. They could pick some and she could make a crumble, but they're both getting fat. Carys has had to buy a new jacket for the funeral because she can't get the buttons done up on her old one.

They pause halfway up the hill, waiting while the dog squeezes out a shit. Carys and Garth talked about getting a dog when Owen left, but Carys wanted to see what her life would be like if she wasn't looking after something or someone. Then Mum had her fall and Owen moved home again, so it was just as well she didn't succumb.

A cluster of women are already gathered in the playground. Carys is relieved to see that some are dressed in outfits as odd as hers, cobbled together from scraps of clothing pulled from the back of a drawer or scraped off a teenager's floor. The women have heavy bodies, as heavy as her sister's and hers. They look like a herd of stout little ponies. One or two among them are slim and tanned—gym bunnies. HRT bunnies. Rich bunnies. Carys recognises one of them from the big house that used to belong to the farm on the other side of the village. She's suddenly self-conscious about her fat fanny in her mother's nylon trousers. She clasps her hands in front of her crotch and looks around for her sister. Sara is over the other side of the playground, settling Billy next to the wall of the school that used to be painted with a mural. The mural has disappeared and in its place are a metre rule, a goal, and a painted target. There are flowerbeds and a sign reading *Edible Garden* where the monkey bars used to be, bark chippings underneath a new climbing frame.

A young woman is in charge. She's tall and she wears her hair in a ponytail that swings from side to side, not unlike the stick lady's on the leaflet. Her sports clothing is tight-fitting and her trainers look properly supportive. She unties a sack made of netting and several balls tumble out on to the tarmac.

'Catch!'

Carys snatches her hand away from her crotch and catches a ball Stick Lady throws to her. She brings the ball close to her face, sniffing it. Its smell of new rubber makes her feel nervous. Sara comes to stand next to her, glancing over at Billy who stares at them from across the playground.

Stick Lady addresses the group, asking if any of them have any injuries or health concerns.

'Have you got a cure for old age?' jokes one of the women.

Stick Lady laughs lightly and explains the three second rule and the stepping rule. While she's talking, Carys clasps the ball tightly and transfers her weight from one side of her body to the other, wondering which is her landing foot. The playground mural used to show two hands holding a green and blue globe, and as she balances the ball between her fingertips, feeling its cool, pimpled surface, she has the whole world in her hands.

'Hello?'

Someone was speaking.

'She wants the ball,' Sara says. Her face is close and there are creases around her eyes and mouth—how old her sister is! The roots of her hair are showing grey, yet they were girls only moments ago.

Stick Lady is asking her to throw the ball, but she can't. She must never let it go. She gazes around the playground, as if seeing it for the first time. There's the cherry tree, whose blossom they would gather to make 'perfume' at lunchtime, there's the entrance to the school, where Sara would wait for her because their mother told her to. There's Sara's dog, lying flat to the ground, his coat the same mixture of greys and browns as the bark chippings, the bricks, the clouds.

She can hear Sara scolding Billy, then realises it's her she is scolding.

'Give her the ball, you numpty!'

'Never mind,' Stick Lady says, picking another ball out of the net bag and throwing it to someone else. Carys is handed a red cotton bib with white letters printed on it. She places the ball carefully on the ground to pull the bib over her head. She fastens the Velcro tabs. Goal Attack.

She crosses the playground to take up her position in the goal half. A whistle blows, and suddenly there's movement. Someone yells and in a panic she looks up as the ball flies towards her. It grazes her fingertips as she fumbles it and the other side gain possession. It's gone in a flash, zigzagging between the players in blue bibs towards the opposite goal. They shoot and score. The woman who called out throws her arms to her sides in frustration—she is one of the ones wearing proper sports clothes—but never mind, Carys is alive to it now, bouncing on her toes, leg muscles pinging as the whistle shrills once more and the women's faces all around her take on a keenness and a focus that wasn't there before. Their eyes glitter and their bodies are alert, animal-like. They are hounds in a race, huntresses after a kill. The ball darts from one pair of hands to another. Carys blazes her way after it, leaving a trace in the air behind her, like a sparkler on fireworks night, or a dragon, flames streaking out all around her. The ball comes to her, she snatches at it, steps once then releases it forwards and Sara is there to catch it, ducking to one side of another woman's body as the woman jumps in front of her. The ball is gone again, firing up to the other end of the pitch, darting among the players. Carys watches as one of the red bibs aims at the hoop and the ball totters then drops and the women raise their voices in a cheer. Sara looms up in front of her once more, panting and laughing, lifting her hand to slap Carys's. Their fingers briefly interlock before they drop hands and return to their designated positions. Mum should see this, see her daughters leaping and throwing and catching and calling. See them playing as part of a team, setting the court on fire.

At the end of the match, everyone is red faced and breathing hard, talking in loud voices about how good that felt.

Sara whistles to Billy and tells him what a good boy he is. 'Aren't you?' she says, bending to rest her face against the dog's slender neck. 'Aren't you?' The dog turns his face to hers, burying his muzzle in her hair, and lets out a shuddering sigh.

They walk back to their mother's house along the lane and down the hill. Sara is humming and Carys picks up her tune.

'It would take a coal miner,' she sings.

'To find her vagina,' sings Sara, and they join their voices for the chorus.

'For the hairs on her dicky-dido hang down to her knees!'

They sing the song over and over, their voices raucous in the chilly air. Billy weaves ahead of them, his patches of white showing up in the growing twilight. A bright moon rises behind the houses, and Carys can feel its light in her chest and in her throat—a fiery glow radiating through her body. They walk along the main road home, like they did when they were girls—knocking on the front door for Mum to open it and let them in.

Garth is waiting in his car, parked in the street outside the house.

'Are you drunk?' he asks, as he and Sara wait for Carys to slot her key in the lock.

'Not yet,' Sara says.

'Where have you been?' he asks, following the women into the house.

'She's cooked, don't worry,' Sara says.

Once they're inside and Carys has switched on the lights, Garth glances at his wife, taking in her strange outfit, her beetroot cheeks, her podgy camel toe.

'Where have you been?' he asks once more, following them into the kitchen.

Billy gulps noisily at the water in his bowl, and before she answers her husband, Carys leans over the sink, ducking her head under the tap to guzzle water. She makes as much noise as the dog, and when she's finished drinking, she splashes water on her face and leans against the sink.

'Where have you been?' her husband asks for a third time.

She wipes her wet hands on the dog, patting him on his skinny back.

'Netball practice,' she says, and the sisters laugh.

The Sparrow

I DEAD-HEAD the rose on the front path as I hurry to the car, snatching at its pistil and ending up with a fistful of petals. At least there'll be more time for gardening after today. I put the key in the car ignition and sprinkle the petals into my lap. Hotels nowadays have rose-petal-strewn beds. I might take myself off to one, one of these days.

Roadworks on the bridge. As the traffic starts to slow, I remember roses climbing in the village where I worked as a community midwife, back in the early days. Would David be surprised to see me now, consulting at his old hospital? Probably not. Even if he was, he wouldn't say anything. Shame he couldn't be more proud. Then again, they say we marry our fathers, and Daddy was the same.

'Couldn't be more proud' is an odd phrase. I test it out loud as I move down the gears, slowing to a stop. I pull up the handbrake. It's not a phrase David would have used. 'Couldn't be more proud' is an expression of a surfeit of pride, and that wasn't David. It wasn't Daddy's way, either. I assumed it would please my father to have me follow him into medicine, and at a time when there were far fewer women doctors than there are now, but he was more concerned with Howard and *his* career, for all the good that did either of them. It will be good to have more time for my brother after today. I stroke the petals in my lap, brushing them off my skirt and on to the floor of the car. The 'Doctor's Only' parking bay gets the morning sun, so they'll smell like potpourri as they dry. A shop selling beauty products made from natural ingredients has opened up in the village and they have trays of flower petals drying in the window. Maybe I'll treat myself. I stroke a stray remaining petal that lies in my lap, finding it satisfying, the way it curls around the pad of my finger tip, silken and smooth. Traffic ahead starts to move, so I release the handbrake, shift the car into first.

When I reach the hospital, I park in my designated spot and swap my driving shoes for work ones. Will I hang on to my work clothes and shoes? A charity shop would be glad of them, but maybe I'll have a need for a sober outfit or two—for what, I don't know.

On any other day the thud of the car's automatic locking system is reassuring, but today it is the sound of gates coming down, of drawbridges being closed.

Nadia greets me with a tilt of her head, and a soft tone in her voice, as if someone has died. Inside the sanctuary of my office, I stand for a moment and survey the space that has housed my professional identity for all this time: a desk and three chairs, a computer, a black leather desk diary, a box of tissues. I know there are no appointments, but I open the diary anyway, at the black ribbon that marks the day, like I have every day for nigh on twenty years. Nadia has tried to convince me to use her electronic calendar, mocking me in her sweet manner for what she calls my 'analogue ways'. But her system would be no good in an earthquake or a flood, would it? Give me my proper diary any day of the week. More than once, Nadia has pointed out that the risk of the hospital's database going down is far more likely than a flood or an earthquake. Each time, I say, 'I rest my case.' And I whisper these words now, alone in my office.

Last day at work! I have written under today's date, my writing as clear and bold as it was when Mr Robinson commended me on it all those years ago. The exuberance of that exclamation mark feels misplaced, though. 'I rest my case,' I whisper, as I close the diary.

Nadia brings the post. Among the internal mail are two plain white envelopes that have come from outside. They will be birth announcement cards, which arrive at regular intervals. If there was a graph showing the rate at which these cards arrive and the pattern of fertility consultations I have held over the past twenty years, the shape of the lines on the graph would likely be the same.

The handwriting on the first white envelope is chubby and round. The card inside has a photograph of a sleeping baby on the front, peaceful and benign as Buddha. The words *Welcoming Noah* are printed above the image. In the card, a handwritten message from the baby's mother. I can't remember her and that makes me feel ashamed. So many patients pass through the clinic, but these people are individuals and I feel bad that this couple and their story haven't stayed with me. Maybe it is time to retire…

I won't take up bridge or golf like others do. I don't under-stand this obsession of hitting balls into holes. Thank goodness David wasn't a golfer. For all his faults, at least he wasn't a golf bore. When I bumped into Anthony Beecham at the opening of the new wing last year, he tried to convince me it was being out in the fresh air and the landscape he appreciated, but that didn't wash. 'What's to stop you going for a nice country walk,' I asked him, 'without this incessant need for goals and targets?' He didn't have an answer. Silly man. More than one negligence case to his name.

I open a drawer and take out a pin tack, hold the card against the felt of the office noticeboard and press the point of the tack through the baby's forehead, adding it to the array of tiny hands and tight little sleeping faces, all the pairs of twins enfolded with one another, as they would have enfolded one another in the womb. *Welcome to the world—Hello!—Just to let you know…* I'll leave them up—a testament to my life's work. Nadia can dispose of them after I've gone.

The second white envelope is a *Happy Retirement* card from a colleague in another part of the country. A widower. Nice of him to remember. I'll take this one home and it will go with the others on the mantelpiece, for now. I'll take them down tomorrow—it feels maudlin to keep them.

I can hear Nadia fielding calls from the reception desk outside the office, informing new patients that Doctor Godwin has retired and is no longer available for appointments. I stare out of the window across the hospital forecourt to the busy ring road and the roundabout beyond the car park. Is this what the future holds? Staring out of the window with nothing to do?

I make a few calls, shred a few remaining documents, chat with Nadia, and visit colleagues in their offices. Most people are busy, so there's only time for a brief chat, and a hug from the best of them. Somehow, I make it through the morning, and when at last I can respectably call the hour lunchtime, I sign off with Nadia in the usual way. She asks if I would like company, offering to come with me on my break. We've always got along. She knew that last week's party was hell for me, just something to get through for the sake of others, for the sake of custom. She apologised about the flowers and the present, giving me the heads up beforehand. We had a laugh afterwards at how convincing my 'surprised' face was. 'You should have been an actor,' she said. I like the way young people don't say actress any more. Actor, actress, what's the difference? It's all an act. If I was going into clinical practice now, I might specialise in gender reassignment cases—that strikes me as interesting work. Imagine what Daddy would have had to say about that. Or David, for that matter. He always was a conservative, with a small c.

Leaving the building to go out for lunch is for appearance's sake, but it does provide an opportunity to breathe some fresh air—though the city's traffic means the air isn't as fresh as it might be. I buy an egg sandwich from Marksies. I'll keep one half and eat it tomorrow. 'You couldn't keep a bird alive on the amount you eat, Mum!' Ruth says. This is how it starts. The beginning of the end.

Ruth's birthday next week. Next door to Marks & Spencer there's a shop that sells greetings cards. The cards are arranged in sections according to the occasion they mark. In this morbid mood, I am drawn to the 'In Sympathy' ones, embossed with lilies and silver crosses. I pause in front of the display, opening a few to read their messages of grief and loss, then scold myself for being melodramatic. Nadia's right, I should have been an actor. I move hastily along the rows of cards, thumbing through birthday greetings. One I open plays a tune, rupturing the quiet of the shop and causing another customer to glance sideways. I take my purchase to the till. No, I don't need a bag, thank you. I slip the card into my handbag alongside the ink fountain pen presented by my colleagues.

It's the end of summer and the leaves are already beginning to turn. The park is especially beautiful at this time of year. The fountain is still going. Come October they'll turn it off. A smell of roasting peanuts catches at the back of my throat. I lift a hand, greeting the peanut seller. We have never spoken, though we see each other most days, and we always wave to each other like this. Will he miss me? Will he even notice I'm gone? There's nothing to stop me visiting the park after I've stopped working—to walk a dog, perhaps. Will I be the kind of woman to get a dog? Is a dog the same as golf?

I sit on a bench to eat my sandwich. I must look like a lonely old woman. Is that what I am? Today, if I'm honest, I do feel a little lonely, though I don't feel old. My thoughts drift to a boy I slept with when I was at medical school. He was studying French. When I googled him, a few years ago, I found out he had written a book, and he was dead. Perhaps I'll order his book. I'll have more time for reading now. How would it have been if we had married? Ruth wouldn't exist.

I take out the birthday card and unscrew the cap on my new pen. A couple stroll past with a small child on a scooter, the father dragging it along by a strap. David taught Ruth how to ride a bicycle. 'Don't let go!' she shouted, and he didn't.

Happy Birthday, dearest daughter. My new pen hovers —what else is there to say? I smooth the card, pressing it flat on to my lap with the palm of my hand. Perhaps now I am retired I no longer have anything to say to anyone, including my own daughter. And me, I laugh, the sound escaping my mouth, who used to have so much to say for myself!

'They wouldn't believe it, would they?' I say out loud, as I shove the card back in my handbag.

They. Colleagues, family members, schoolfriends. I had a reputation for speaking my mind. Got me into trouble on more than one occasion. I glance around, checking to see if anyone has noticed me laughing and talking to myself. No one's eye is on the sparrow, though. No one notices an old woman on a park bench, no matter how well-preserved she is.

'Well-preserved' is what that nincompoop said at that party last year. As if I was a wine or a cheese, something consumable. I will not be consumed.

I walk on to the next empty bench, which looks out over the skate park. Sitting down, I slip off my shoes. The tops of my feet are marked with welts where the leather has pressed into the thin skin. Skin thinning all over my body as I dry into a blonde husk. Soon I will cease to chafe (oh, the chafing. Praise God and the pharmas for vaginal pessaries) and I will be chaff. I lean forwards to massage one foot and then the other.

A young man is whirling around the concrete slopes on his skateboard with a small girl tucked under his legs. She can only be about three or four years old. He's holding her hands and with the grace of an ice skater, he leans into the curves, as they glide smoothly around. The skateboard wheels whirr as they pass by. The little girl's face and body are a miniature facsimile of the young man's—he must be her father. The momentum the weight of their two bodies creates carries them away from me. It is a beautiful sight.

The skateboard rolls to a halt in front of a huddle of other skinny lads. 'Did you like that, Ruby?' one of them asks the girl.

Several Rubys among the birth announcement cards I've received in recent years. Funny, how the old-fashioned names have come back.

The Sparrow

So many babies I help to bring into the world whose destinies I never get to know about, so many stories I began whose endings I never hear. And now mine is coming to a close—how will it end? Retirement can be a new beginning... But enough of the schlocky greetings card sentiment. Work has been a distraction, and truth be told, I'm a little envious of David—and others who have gone. Death, like birth, is something to be got through and he's done his labour already. He has crossed to the other side and the ordeal of it, the hard slog of it, is over. Mine still to come.

Would it be too much to thank the widower for his card? A telephone call too presumptuous. Though it would be easy enough for Nadia to find his number.

The skateboarder lifts the girl gently on to the ground. He reaches into a rucksack lying nearby and hands her a plastic beaker to drink from. She holds it with two hands. I want to tell the young man—he's a boy, really—what a good job he's doing. I put my shoes back on and stand from the bench. The leather pinches. A smell of marijuana drifts on the air. I hover at the edge of the park, my heart racing as I am about to open my mouth—and say what, exactly? Maybe just an observation of how much the little girl seemed to enjoy the skateboarding? One of the youths glances over and I move on.

The peanut seller smiles and lifts a hand as I head back towards the gates. I wave back. One day I might even buy some peanuts from him. And some marijuana from the teenage father, while I'm at it. Retirement can be a time for letting go of everything I've been holding together until now. Peanuts and Mary Jane for me, instead of dogs and golf.

A loud hooting and a screech of brakes. A driver gestures rudely. The signal for pedestrians was still red. I raise a hand in apology and disarm the driver with a smile that I bring to my face from the centre of me, hauling it up like a bucket from a well. He flicks a hand, hits the accelerator and his car emits a puff of dirty smoke from its exhaust as it hurtles around the corner.

I have lost a shoe. Someone stoops to pick it up. I thank them and the person holds out their arm so I can lean on them as I slide the shoe back on, pressing my heel firmly inside the leather, before putting one foot in front of the other and making my way across the road towards the kerb on the opposite side.

Granny's Gun

MAMAN IS KNOCKING back the wine and flirting with everyone. Bella stands at the glass doors separating the living room from the kitchen, watching her mother weaving among the guests, getting into conversations with people who will tell Bella afterwards what a lovely lady her mother is, how chic, in her smartly tailored jacket and bobbed hair, how like a small exotic bird, with her continental style and her accent.

She has invited too many parents. It feels more like an afternoon piss-up than a kids' party, with Maman doing most of the drinking. She's chattering away to Alek now, laughing while slyly topping up her glass from a bottle someone has tucked behind the Death Star on top of the piano. Did she stash the bottle there herself? The top of her head only reaches Alek's chest and she's talking fast. What is she saying to him? She's never made a secret of the fact that she wished she'd had sons instead of daughters.

'She's a man's woman, not a woman's woman,' Bella tells her friend, Neeta.

'Oh, but she's so chic, look at her! She reminds me of a little bird.'

Bella tops up both their glasses.

'Children's parties are so stressful,' Neeta says.

'Tell me about it. I had to have a shag before you lot turned up, to calm me down.'

Neeta spits out her wine as she laughs. 'You didn't! How did you have time?' She gestures around the room at the party decorations, the spider webs strung from the ceiling, the cardboard cut-outs of superheroes—which Bella has spent the last week making—stuck to the walls.

'Well, it wasn't really a shag, was it, darling?' Bella turns to her husband, Alek, who has just come into the kitchen.

'What?' He joins them at the glass doors.

'Just a quick finger. He probably still smells of me.' Bella snatches her husband's hand and holds it under her friend's nose.

'Ew, Bel-la!' Neeta pulls sharply away. Then says, 'You're a lucky man, Al.'

Neet has always fancied Alek.

'More to the point, where were the kids?'

All three of them spot Ivan as he darts into the front room, looking for something, or someone.

'Ivan was busy destroying the piñata,' Alek says, 'and Ollie went down for his nap.'

Not finding whatever it is he's looking for, Ivan pushes through the adult bodies and comes up against his granny.

Maman bends to whisper something in his ear and he shrinks from her Sauvignon breath. She has surprising strength for such a tiny woman, though, and she grips him hard, keeping him where she wants him. She is doubtless encouraging him in the kind of behaviour that has had Bella invited up to the school for a 'chat' on more than one occasion.

'Time for the cake, do you think?' Alek asks.

'In a minute…hang on.' Bella keeps Ivan in her sights as his granny leads him to a corner of the room. She can see him tearing open the present Maman has given him. He glances up as soon as he has the thing in his hand, and catching sight of his mother watching him, he pushes through the party, crashing towards her.

'Fucking Mum!' Bella curses.

'What's she done now?' Alek asks. He's putting candles on the cake.

'Wait till you see what she's given him.'

Alek glances up as their son barges into the kitchen brandishing a plastic machine gun. Neeta lifts her glass of wine into the air, capping it with the palm of her hand.

'Mum, look what granny gave me!'

'Oh, wow, Ivan. That's fantastic.' Bella won't give her mother the satisfaction of showing how annoyed she is. 'What do you say?' she says, instead.

Her boy turns to his grandmother, who has followed him into the kitchen. 'Thank you, Mamie.'

'Mer-ci,' Maman corrects him.

'Merci.'

Bella and her mother exchange glances. Maman's eyes glitter dangerously.

'One day you will 'ave a real gun, Ivan,' she says, 'and I will take you shooting rabbits.'

115

'Shoot them dead?' Ivan asks.

'Cake now!' Bella sings, and she yells through the glass doors, 'Cake everyone! Turn the lights off!'

Ivan legs it out of the kitchen, yelling that his cake is ready.

'I thought you said it was a spider, Isabelle?' Maman says, leaning over the cake Bella was making late into the night. 'It looks more like un canard.'

'No, it's definitely a spider, Mum.'

Maman shrugs and begins a tour of the kitchen, looking for more wine. Bella flicks two fingers up at her mother's back, then hooks an arm around Neeta's shoulders and draws her close, hissing in her ear, 'You know the old two fingers is what the English showed the French at Agincourt, right?' She releases her friend and heaves a dramatic sigh. 'Did you see what she gave him?'

'I saw. It's not going to help,' Neeta says.

They stand at the glass doors watching Ivan spraying the adult guests with noisy gunfire. His friends, including Neeta's boy, who has been the victim of Ivan's 'boisterous' behaviour on more than one occasion, gather around him, clamouring for a go. He turns the gun on them, too.

'Talk about family history repeating itself,' Bella says, turning back to help Alek with the cake.

'What do you mean?' Alek asks, tearing open the cellophane on a packet of Spiderman napkins and handing them to her.

'Maman. Surely you've heard the one about the doll her Papie bought her?'

'Don't think I know that one,' Alek says. 'Where are the matches?'

'Oh, listen to this, Neet,' Bella says, grabbing her friend's arm as she's about to leave the kitchen, 'you're going to love it. Mamie's family were strict Catholics, right? So when Maman's

116

grandad bought her a beautiful doll, it was deemed too extravagant for a little girl and they took her to the shop and made her give it back.'

Bella can see the scene in her mind's eye, her mother has described it so often and so vividly: tiny Cecile handing the beloved doll to the shop man and receiving several notes in return, which the shop man smoothed out flat before giving to her, and which her mother folded away in her black snippy-snappy purse. Maman told and retold the tale throughout Bella's childhood, on every occasion that Bella received a precious gift. 'I was five years old, a leetle girl only,' she would cry, still outraged after seventy years.

'Well, I'll break the cycle of fuck-uppery,' Bella says. 'Ivan can have the gun.'

The lights on the baby monitor flicker as Ivan's little brother Ollie wakes up from his nap. Bella makes a grab for Alek's arm and bites it so hard he drops the matches. Neeta lets out a startled gasp.

'Sometimes I just have to chow down on something,' Bella says. 'Do you get that?'

Neeta shakes her head.

'It's alright, it doesn't hurt,' Alek reassures her, rubbing away his wife's teeth marks.

He bends to pick matches off the floor.

The following week, Ivan's teacher takes Bella to one side at home time.

'Ivan brought a gun into school today,' she begins, and she widens her eyes at Bella.

'It was a present from his grandmother, sorry—'

'It's school policy not to allow toys of this kind,' the teacher says.

A pencil pot on a shelf behind Ms Pettifer declares her the *World's Best Teacher*.

'I completely understand. I'm sorry, it won't happen again.'

Ms Pettifer reaches under her desk to retrieve the toy gun, handing it to Bella in silence. Bella slides it under her coat, like a character from Bugsy Malone.

'As you know,' Ms Pettifer says, 'Ivan's class are due to visit a city farm on Friday. But attendance on school trips is dependent on good behaviour. Perhaps you could reinforce this message at home?'

Bella assures Ms Pettifer she will, and she leaves to collect Ollie and Ivan from the playground where they are swarming over the climbing frame with Neeta's boys, while Neeta watches them.

Later that evening, Bella tells Ivan that he can only go to the farm if he is good.

'But I want to go to the farm,' her boy whispers, not taking his eyes from the programme he's watching on television. His hair is damp from the bath and he's wearing his new Spiderman pyjamas.

'And you can go, Spidey-Ivey, if you're a good boy.'

He turns to face her.

'But I want to go the farm!'

'You can do it,' Bella urges him. 'You can be a good boy.'

'No, I can't!' he yells, in an ugly, splitting voice.

Through the glass doors, she can see Ollie naked, apart from a nappy, emptying a bag of flour over the kitchen floor.

'Shoot me,' Ivan begs her, throwing off his blanket and standing on the sofa. 'Shoot me in the heart! I want to die!'

'Come and have a cuddle.'

Ivan shakes his head wildly, pushing past her and running upstairs.

It's not his fault. It's her fault for naming him after a Russian despot. People are too quick to joke about him living up to his name, 'Ivan the Terrible'.

No, it's not her fault and it's not Ivan's fault, Bella thinks. She knows whose fault it is. She snatches up the phone and punches in her mother's number. She'll tell her how upset her grandchild is because of her and her thoughtlessness, because of her and her ideas about what makes a good present for a six-year-old. She can hear Ivan smashing things up in his bedroom. In the kitchen, Ollie sifts flour through his fingers, enjoying the soft powdery mess he has made.

'It's all your fault, you stupid, stupid woman!' Bella screams into the phone.

Ollie stares at her, transfixed.

'Isabelle? What's my fault? Is Aleksander leaving you?'

'No!' She tells her mother about Ivan's threatened exclusion from the farm trip, while Ollie shuffles over to her on his bottom, hauling himself up to standing by pulling on her clothes with his floury little hands.

'I don't know what you are shouting about. Teachers, pff! Idiotes,' her mother says, when Bella has finished. 'Of course Ivan will go to ze farm.'

'That's not the point, Mum! The point is…the point is—'

'Oui, Isabelle, what is ze point?'

Bella throws down the phone and watches it skid across the floor. She gnashes her teeth, looking around for something to bite on. Ollie's podgy arm, lightly dusted with white up to the elbow, is as succulent and yielding as Turkish delight.

Her baby looks surprised, more than anything, that she would hurt him like that. Then he screams.

'Oh, Ollie—' Sick with panic, she gathers him and holds him tight, walking him up and down with his shrill screams piercing her ears. She sits on the stairs with him, rocking backwards and forwards and screwing her eyes shut, while her teeth marks bloom in an ugly welt on his milky skin.

'What happened?' Ivan emerges from his bedroom. His face is pink and he is naked. He comes to stand at the top of the landing. 'What happened to Ollie?'

When she doesn't answer and Ollie doesn't stop crying, Ivan treads carefully down the stairs and puts his arms around them. They stay still for a long time, until Alek arrives home from work and finds them.

Ivan is allowed to go on the class trip. His teacher blushingly informs Bella that, while he hasn't really earned his place, she thinks it would be unfair to exclude him, and could Bella please sign a risk assessment form for the day.

At the farm, on his best behaviour, Ivan clings to Ms Pettifer's side, while Bella clings to Ollie. A sow has recently given birth and everyone gathers by the stall to watch her suckle her babies, their pipe-cleaner tails twitching in the straw. Bella sees her give one of the babies a nip when it jostles its siblings. She holds Ollie closer, willing him to be as nonchalant about his mother's behaviour as the little piglet. Maman wasn't—isn't—such a terrible mother, she thinks, as she leans over the pigsty wall. At least she never bit me.

'Shall we call on Mamie?' she asks her boys, on the drive home afterwards, and Ivan pronounces this his best day ever.

Connie and Me

A MESSAGE IS LEFT on our landlord's answering machine.

'This is Connie,' the voice says. '…I need a favour.'

The voice is English, but sounds strange—like no other I have ever heard—with long pauses between each word, and each word taking great effort. 'Could you possibly lend us ten pounds, dear?' the voice says. 'So we can buy ourselves some food… If you could phone me back, I'd be very grateful.'

I replay the message to Jie when he gets home from university. We ring the number and explain we have received the phone call by mistake.

'That's right, dear,' says the same voice we heard in the message. 'We've got no food to eat, and no money to buy any with.'

I ask for her address and she gives it to me.

Jie drops off some money on this first occasion, handing it over to a woman, he tells me, when he gets back. He doesn't tell me anything else. The next day, Connie rings my number to say how grateful she is and what a good-looking young man my husband is. I don't correct her, even though Junjie is not my husband.

'I'm always happy to have visits from handsome gentlemen,' she says, 'of whatever creed or colour.'

I ask her the meaning of the word 'creed'. It's not a word I've come across.

'Religion, dear.'

She tells me she believes in God. I tell her I do, too. She tells me I am her guardian angel.

The next time she rings, a few weeks later, she asks us to collect a cheque in payment for the money she borrowed. Jie is studying, so I go to her home. The building Connie lives in is Regency style, divided into flats. I ring one of the many bells, and after some time, a woman opens the heavy front door. She is enormous, with a speckled face and stiff grey hair styled upwards like a 1950s rock and roll star. She wears a white sweater, decorated with pearls and sequins and a brown stain.

'Ooh, aren't you lovely,' she says. 'Like a little doll!'

She invites me inside her home. It smells of cigarette smoke and is crowded with broken furniture. The carpets are threadbare and the walls are streaked and stained. Tissue boxes are stuffed with used tissues. There is a blue leather-look armchair with a worn patch in the middle of the seat. Several dusty VHS cases lay on the floor next to an old-fashioned television.

'Tell me your name, again,' Connie says.

She is so wide and tall she fills the small apartment.

'Mèi-Mei,' I tell her.

'May I?' she says, and she tells me it's her little joke as she hands me a crumpled cheque. It is written in curly handwriting and post-dated by a few weeks, if we don't mind? We chat for a little while, and I discover she lives with Roger, a window cleaner, who is out shopping. She has a sister nearby, the best sister in the world.

Connie phones to ask if we have paid her cheque in yet. She is relieved to hear that we haven't. She warns me it's no good—can I destroy it, please, and she'll write me another? I assure her we do not need her to pay us back, that we can afford to give her the money, but she is insistent. I visit her a second time to collect a new cheque.

Connie phones every couple of months after that, asking to borrow money for food. We deliver cash—ten pounds, mostly, sometimes twenty or thirty. She gives us cheques, which she will later inform us are 'no good'. Sometimes phone calls include further requests for money. When I visit her, she tells me I look lovely, admires my flower rucksack, the pom-pom on my keyring. When I tell her that she, too, is lovely, she thanks me for the compliment. She makes a note of our birthdays and presses gifts on me—Dove soap, Robertson's Golden Shred marmalade. At Chinese New Year, I give her a red envelope, and she gives me a porcelain thimble with a windmill painted on it.

Occasionally, Roger is present when I visit. He is a giant, with big hands that he holds awkwardly in front of his body. If he makes conversation, it is to tell me how ladylike I am, and what a lovely figure I have. He wants to put me in his pocket. Connie tells me she used to be a model. She has photographs that she will show me some time. I tell her I would like that.

She signs off our telephone calls with, 'Love you!' and 'God bless.' I tell her I love her, too. I treasure her friendship. My family are far away and I have not been home since starting my Master's Degree, so it is a pleasure for me to say. It is not something I say too often with my family, or with Jie.

It is true, I love her.

One day, I encounter her coming down the steps with another woman. She introduces her as her sister, Helen. Helen is a big, spreading woman, like Connie—they are mirror images, more like twins, except Connie is in slippers and wears stained and dirty clothes, while Helen is clean and neatly dressed. Connie doesn't look well. She suffers with her legs, Helen explains, and Connie lifts her skirt showing shiny open sores on each ankle.

She continues to phone. On Junjie's birthday she calls several times throughout the day to sing 'Happy Birthday'. I tell her he is studying and she asks me to get him to call back.

'How are your legs, Connie?' I ask.

'Better, thank you,' she says. 'I can put my shoes on. I'm going for a walk to celebrate.'

When Jie rings her back, he puts her on speaker and she sings 'For He's a Jolly Good Fellow'.

One Christmas, she invites us for tea and lemonade. Jie doesn't want to go and is relieved when Connie cancels only a few hours before we are due. She confesses she sometimes gets 'a bit down', and when she's low, she doesn't feel like seeing anyone.

I receive a call from her sister. We've been so kind, Helen says, could we do another small favour and not lend Connie money?

'Without going into it,' she says, 'there has been financial abuse.'

But she does go into it. Helen is applying for power of attorney. Roger has been inciting Connie to ask for money, then gambling it. Helen says Connie has been forced to live in poverty. 'You've seen the way they live,' she says. 'There's no need for it'. She very much wants to pay us back the money Connie owes us. I tell her it is not necessary.

Connie continues to call, but we deny her softly, softly. I begin to visit her without delivering cash or receiving cheques. This morning she is wearing a red and white polka-dot dress, glimpses of her body visible where she hasn't done up the buttons properly. She seems sleepy, talking slowly, searching for words—a result of medication, maybe. She has an abscess on her eye.

I ask about the modelling photos she told me about. I do not expect her to have them, but with no hesitation she points out an ancient brown envelope on the coffee table. I sit on the floor next to her chair. There is a patch of what looks like dried vomit on the carpet. It doesn't smell—too old, maybe, or the smell of cigarettes masking it. I open the envelope. Inside are black and white contact sheets, showing a slim young woman in ski pants and polo-necked sweater swinging on the metal steps of a fire escape, smiling at the camera. She peeks out from between the bars of a roundabout, kneels on a fallen tree, poses against a sea wall in a bikini, splashes in the shallows. She has a lovely smile. She is unmistakably Connie.

I sneak a glance at my friend. She supports her head with one hand and rubs at her hair with the other. Her hair is that of an old person, nothing like the glossy ponytail in the pictures. She leans forward so her face is close to mine. Her abscessed eye half closed, she smiles shyly and asks, 'Do you think I've changed much?'

3 o'clock

3 o'clock   hates it if I'm late   no rushing though   take my time

Hands along the back of the sofa patting the slippy blanket
   back into place then chair at the table clanking my mug
   against its hard wood like school climbing equipment when
   I was a girl shinning up the rungs of those ladders like I was
   born for it

                              unladylike but I didn't care

told off for whistling
               what's wrong with a whistle? Cheerful.

   Door frame now and try a whistle before crossing the bright
   space of the kitchen to the sink

Cold shiver of the draining board under my hands
                                    pretty hands always.

Ladylike.

Brightness of the kitchen lights blink

        rinse out my mug—cup not face—and put it away.

Whiteness of fridge inside and a blast of cold. *Close the door,
it costs me money every time you go in there!* and because of
him saying that I can't help thinking of someone sitting there
like one of his little gnomes only instead of a fishing rod he's
got some kind of accounts book like the one I used to
keep and he adds to his sums every time I open the door

                        A square of dark.
                        Who put it there?

Hands back along the chair at the table
            climbing the school ladders and sitting at the top like
                    monkeys in a tree.

Sofa

No rushing, take my time like Angela's always saying. *All the
time in the world, Mum, don't worry.* So little time, though,
when everything takes longer. Smart bag, leather, zip unzip.
Check for purse. Splash of red, one Christmas. A good purse,
cost a pretty penny, I bet. Don't waste your money on me.

3 o'clock

A square of dark on the wall in here too getting on my nerves
                    clean it off when I've time but so little time
         when everything takes longer
                    draw the curtains around it so I can't see it.

Smart bag. Purse. Coat. Blessed buttons. Him always so
smart. His mother and sister, too. *You could wear the same
outfit, Clem, and it wouldn't look so smart.* Never mind.

                                        Deadlocking the door
                              like that other one showed me
                    and look down to see no __ Bare legs
              only, and those not a pretty sight. Jesus,
         Mary and Joseph. Fiddling with the blessed lock
    and indoors once more to fetch— What are they called?
No matter. *Not to worry, Mum, it's not important.* Important
to dress well, though. Appearance is important and he likes
me to look nice. Smart bag. Put it down and pick it up again
like Sukey with that blessed kettle. No time for a cup, not
without __ on, but they do a nice cuppa there. Him always
so smart and me with my legs out like a hussy.

                    Carpet soft between my toes like—stuff you
      get on holiday. Should have known I didn't have whatsits on
because of the feel of the carpet, silly goose. Maybe a little
lie down only not in my coat and all the buttons only just
fastened plus he'll be on time. He'll have had a shave, when?
I'll ask him and he'll tell me to guess. You guess, he'll say,
and he'll give me his cheek to stroke right there and then.
Soft as a baby's bum, bit rude, and there's that cheek of his
again, under my fingers and in the air all around.

Me on the low chair next to the bed with my coat and bag
   on and him waiting for me, dear God. Off with one shoe and
   then the other, hard at the best of times but especially in my
   wool coat, buttons done. 'Getting old, Clem,' and my voice
   loud in the quiet. Talking to yourself now, are we?

Something written next to the bed, telling me something but
   I don't know what. So much information. But legs the
   main thing, and their coverings— What's the word? Sorted
in the drawer and all the ones with holes in thrown
out when Angela came. Angela, like an angel, which is
   what we said when we decided.

Pretty feet, Bill always said.

      Hard as hooves and cold in bed against his warm legs.

   Fiddly business, rolling on the stockings—stockings, that's
it. Tights, now I've got it, no stopping me now and buses,
   willing, are not late either. Limp like the skin a whatsit
leaves behind when it grows out of it. Snake. Careful not
to ladder the blessed things, slightly gravelly between the
fingers, grains like— stuff you get on holiday. Same colour
too, American in the old days not now, words like nude,
   Angie says, and there's me going out with my bare legs. *Not
so many streakers as there used to be, was that a fashion
then?* The kind of thing she talks about when she shows me
her magazines, shooting the breeze. What did the breeze do
to you I say and she tells me I've still got it. Haul the things
up around the waist, Gordon Bennett, but I'm not taking it off,
not undoing the buttons I've only just done them up. Smart
bag next to the chair. Purse inside. Coat. *You could wear the
same outfit, Clem*, but tights on and them without a hole so
that's something.

Deadlock and outside cold enough to wake the dead and the
squares of dark all over. Lots of Indians dead, apparently, *and
they'll all be women*, Angela says. *All the people that work in
these places are ladies, Mum, their children asleep under the
machines like in Victorian times. Or working themselves*, so
she says, *sewing footballs*. Reminds me of history, I tell her,
the pigs' bladders they used to kick about in the olden days.
No pigs' bladders in the Premiership, Mum, and gathering
up our afternoon cups she sits down again, when I remember
Bill and his pools coupon, see I haven't lost my marbles quite
yet, plenty left. *Plenty of marbles, Mum*, she says and she's
smiling at me, but with all of her face like him. All of her face
and her whole body, too, not the smile when she's tired and
it only comes from the mouth. Her body slackening now, and
loose like water or gravy, slopping over our own sides.
Whatever happened to that gravy boat we used to have?
Oh, Mum, she says, *I haven't seen that for years, not since
Dad died.*

This square of dark in front—a trick of the light or the
mind playing tricks like the doctor mentioned can happen
sometimes? Like the headaches before Angela was born,
never afterwards, as if she cured me, the angel from heaven
that she is.

Coins for my fare but the bus doesn't come and doesn't come.
Wind whipping and a tightening of my— thing that goes
around my neck   not a scarf   attached to my—Bill's
always filthy until I worked my magic.

Sweat, I suppose. A man's sweat. Collar, that's it.

Wind whipping, wish it would whip away the square of dark,
bat it away like a pesky fly.
Shoo fly, don't bother me, I belong to somebody.

Lights and a slowing but not my usual bus. Where are you
going?   Never used to have lady drivers but here she is. It's
more common now. Out of the window now, this one's asking.
Woolworths, I say, and she tells me Woolworths is closed.
Woolworths, I tell her. He hates it if I'm late. Woolworths
isn't open, it's late, says she. Hates it if I'm late. Do I want
to hop in, but I tell her I'll wait for the bus that takes me right
outside. There's no buses, do you want to hop in?

Hop in, she says, but there's no hopping. Hold on, she
says and here she is, take my arm, take my time. What's that
tinkling sound? Oh, it's me, she says, laughing and she shakes
both her arms, holding them up in the air and shaking them
so all the bracelets jingle and jangle like it's Christmas. She's
pretty sure Woolworths isn't open any more, but she'll take
me there anyway, to have a look.

The same dark square in front—it's a wonder she can see
to drive. In front of us the whole way and she's very chatty,
this one. Not my usual bus and she's got flowers around her
whatsit, thing you drive with. Holds on to it, rings on her
fingers, bells on her toes. Bits of rag tied around her wrists
and in her hair for ringlets in the morning, bangles jangling
whenever she moves her hands. Tattoos, like my name
etched across Bill's fingers, and his own name on the
knuckles of his other hand, like he'd forget it if not.

3 o'clock

Turning wheel.
Steering.

Steering wheel.

One of her bracelets in the shape of a snake clamped around
the top of her arm. Not on her wrist but around the top of her
arm like an Egyptian queen, like Cleopatra, and something on
her head like snakes too, hanging down her back. Bracelets
glinting in the street lights as we pass underneath, driving
fast, giddy. *Beautiful arms, you've got,* Bill used to say.
*Some are breast and some are bum, but me, I'm all about
the arms and legs and you've got a nice set of pins.* Burying
my feet in the— stuff you get. Lots of it, you know. Colour
of whatsit. Golden gets everywhere. Little curtains like
we're in a moving house, like we're in a house driving down
the road. Giddy at the thought of a house moving along at
quite a lick. Giddy like we're on a fairground ride. Smart
bag. Purse. Coat. Him always so smart, and his mother, too.
*You could wear the same outfit, Clem, and it wouldn't look
so smart.* We're just on our way back from a festival, she
says, what's your name, but I don't tell her, best not. Hold
tight, just don't let go of me, Bill, I said. *Close your eyes and
you won't get giddy,* he said, so I did.

It used to be Woolworths,
she says, but they closed down,
she says, and besides, it's late, do
you know what time it is? I don't like to be
late, with him so punctual and good looking. It's
late, she says. It's 3 o'clock in the morning! Shall I take
you home? What's your address? Would I mind if she
looks in my bag? Smart bag, open on my lap. Her hands
inside. Purse. Piece of paper Angela wrote and now both
hands on the steering wheel and around we go like Bill and
me on the Waltzer.

133

Dark square all the way back where we came from.

Sorry it's so high, can you manage?

No talk of hopping

fast, faster up the path

feet on top of one another

     path hits

dark on top of me

     lying looking up

Are you alright? Take my hand, can you hold on to me?

Oh, Bill, where did you? Why did you have to? You know me, he says, I haven't gone far.

You're bleeding, I'm so sorry. Bracelets tinkling as she takes my arm. Is it this one? Looking at the numbers on the doors. Have you got a key? Sorry about your tights.

Indoors makes a cup of something and I find my tongue again. Cat got it. Did you see the little man? Looks confused, she didn't see a man. It costs me money every time you go in there! Sorry, she says, I thought you might want milk in your tea. She's looking around for something.

A pen, she says, and something to write on. Oh this will do.
Do you mind if I write a note on this? What is it? A letter
about the electric, I'll use the back where there's no writing.
Ends of the snakes on her head touch the table as she writes.
It's just a note to explain what happened. Maybe you could
show it to your doctor? Or a relative? Is there someone that
comes? Her warm breath and a smell of bonfires as she
leans forward to give me a hug. Then she is gone and the
jangle of bangles and the bonfires with her. Buttons take ages
and these things will have to come off now they've got a hole
in. Him and his mother so smart. They'll need chucking out
with the rest she threw out—when I can get them off, that is.
Texture between fingertips, tiny grains like sugar and that
trip to the glass factory that Angela went on one time. *You'll
never believe it, Mum,* she said. *Hot as anything and made
out of*— Gets everywhere. Not Brighton where there's
stones so hard they make your bum ache and when you get
up your legs are printed with the marks. Margate where
Bill complimented me on my hourglass figure.

Sand.

G-lorious

AN ALARM SOUNDS, terminals fade and erudites whirr into hir slots: *G-lore is closed now*. Lights dim to lo-glo and the invigorators on upper floors slow to a stop, people step off apparatus and make hir way to exits, checking hir levels as ze head towards the outside.

Hidden in a gap between columns, an elder has fallen asleep. Gloria is dreaming of home. Not hir pretty cottage a link-ride away from G-lore, but the home hir father grew up in, which ze visited once or twice while air travel was still a thing. Ze is dreaming of the shade of the mango trees, chirping tree frogs at night, hir grandmother's laugh, Auntie's cockerel. *G-lore is closing now*, hir auntie is saying. *Apologies, G-lore is closed.*

Gloria opens hir eyes. The chair ze has been sleeping in perfectly contains hir body so ze feels like the tiny girl in a story Daddy used to tell hir, who slept in the middle of a flower and went sailing in a boat made of half a walnut shell.

Ze checks hir imagometer, which is flickering madly. Ze must have been dreaming. Hir G-recol will be through the roof.

G-lore is closing now.

It's not Auntie speaking, it's an erudite, its silly digi-viz in the centre of its structure increasing in brightness as it waits for hir response. *G-lore is closed*, it says, as if it thinks Gloria might not have understood. *Please visit again soon.*

'There's no need to shout,' Gloria says, lashing out with one foot and sending it spinning on its way, like a sycamore seed pod—'helicopters' Gloria's children used to call them.

Through the roof. Hir imagometer logs the new idiom.

Ze has been at G-lore Store all day, while waders have been dealing with a flood in hir kitchen. Water came in during the night. Gloria could hear it trickling when ze woke up. Hir first thought, as ze rose up through sleep, was that Daddy was peeing outside the house. Then ze remembered Daddy was dead. When ze went downstairs, one of hir slip-ons was bobbing next to the back door. Ze couldn't understand its movement at first, or its height, as it hovered above floor level like a drone, and all the while, the sound of water trickling.

Hir neighbour told hir there was a spring behind hir houses. There had never been a flood before. Ze cupped a handful of water, allowing it to trickle through hir fingers.

'Is it real?' Gloria had asked, and because ze is an elder like hir, ze didn't scold hir for hir question—Gloria's daughter and hir G-randchildren perceive no difference between reality and G-reality. Ze always say, 'What does it matter if it's real or G-real?' and ze never has an answer. Hir argument, that if

G-reality feels the same then it is as real as the organic kind, is persuasive, but ze don't understand what it's like to have grown up during an era when there was a difference.

It's dark outside when ze steps on to the rural-link. Hir daughter, Josie, comes through on hir neupath.

—where are you—

—link—

— get off it, you're going to have to sleep the night here—

It isn't the most generous of invitations. Hir daughter doesn't sound happy about having hir to stay, but it turns out there's an obstruction and next-level drainage is required to clear the flood water from hir cottage. Gloria waits for the link to glide to a halt and steps off.

—I see you upped your recol storage today—

This is Josie's way of saying thank you, but ze doesn't actually say the words. People tend not to, these days. Gloria misses that particular custom, but gone are the days when anyone had anything to thank one's elders for. Nevertheless, ze is proud that hir G-recol account is funding hir G-randchildren's edu, and ze is pleased hir dreams and memories are of value, since hir family don't seem interested in them for hir own sake. As currency, though, ze have, well, currency.

Citi-link deposits hir on the threshold of hir daughter's home and ze is admitted.

'Josie?'

Hir voice sounds unnaturally loud in the hushed static of the living space.

'Hello, G-ran.'

Tutz sidles up to hir, extends a hand, which ze brushes against Gloria's shoulder, then lets it drop. At roman-sixteen, ze is Gloria's youngest G-randchild, but ze has more of the old ways than many people. Tutz will be the saviour of this family, Gloria thinks, if not the saviour of the entire human race.

—too kind— Tutz tunes into hir neupath.

There is no privacy any more. Gloria misses private space.

—you're elder, G-ran, of course there are things you miss—

—I know— Gloria responds via neupath, even though ze would much rather speak out loud. Ze is an elder, but ze doesn't feel elderly. Ze feels as ze has always felt. Ze feels roman-fifteen, just as ze felt roman-fifteen when ze was roman-eighty, roman-ninety, a century.

—where's Manni?— ze asks.

Tutz gestures across the calm, pale space to where Manni lies prone on the opiode.

'We can't do a thing with hir,' Josie says out loud, coming into the room. 'Have you eaten? There's food if not.'

'Not,' Gloria answers, and Josie moves to the Haier, bringing out dishes of vegetables and the potatoes ze knows hir mother likes. Gloria sees the alert ze sends Manni, but it is ignored and Josie is reduced to calling out loud, 'Come, Manni! Food.'

Manni wanders over, greeting Gloria with the briefest nod of hir head. When ze were small, G-enealog indicated shared patterns of interest between Gloria and both hir G-randchildren, which generated a decent edattain rating, but Manni isn't interested in edu. That's hir choice, Josie says, and there's not much anyone, least of all Gloria, can do about it if Manni wants to confine hirself to inute. Gloria doesn't think Josie tries hard enough to engage hir child, but ze made the mistake of saying so once, and ze won't do that again. In the past, Manni would have been known as the 'black sheep' of the family, but sheep are long gone, along with men, along with Apis.

Gloria's imagometer flickers. *Black sheep of the family.*

139

'I miss sheep,' ze says out loud.

Ze hauls hirself on to one of the high stools at the Haier, next to a row of pots containing odd-looking plants.

'Are these edible?' ze asks, wondering if ze are herbs of some kind.

'No, Mum.'

Gloria's mind trails back to hir gardening days when Josie was young and hir brother Kit was just a baby. That was back in the days when ze was still with Doug, before hir parents died, even, back in the days when there were still private gardens. Hir employer used to spy on hir breastfeeding, dirty bugger. Hir imagometer registers the memory. What was hir name again? Hir G-recol account will be sky high at this rate. *Sky high*. Something posh. Something so English it was faintly ridiculous, ze remembers, but perhaps ze has got that wrong. Perhaps it was John, or something ordinary like that.

—Richard, wasn't it?— Josie comments via neupath. —I remember coming to hir garden after school sometimes—

'Where was that?' hir daughter asks, out loud.

'Outside citi,' Gloria tells hir. 'Where the storage facility is now. Hir house is still standing, I think.'

Ze was still known as Caro then. Ze took hir G-name like everyone else in the elder G-eneration, when it became expedient to do so. Ze saw what happened to those who didn't, or rather, ze didn't see them… That was the point. Anyone who resisted the G-ynae Revolution disappeared.

Having eaten, Manni wanders back to the opiode. Gloria watches hir body move through the softly lit space, so tender and innocent in its resilience, so aimless.

—are you feeling alright, Mum?—

Gloria wishes ze was at home in hir little cottage.

—you can go home in the morning—

'How do you fancy painting, G-ran?' Tutz says out loud, and Gloria knows hir game. *To know a person's game.* There was a big drive in the twenties to prevent what ze used to call Old People or The Elderly from becoming isolated. Elders need stimulation, everyone knows that now. Enough stimulation already, thinks Gloria. Ze just wants to be left alone.

Josie shares info —visit artist's studio via G-lore—

'I always fancied trying my hand at painting,' Gloria says, throwing them a bone.

Hir imagometer logs *try my hand at* and *to throw someone a bone.* Ze agrees to a painting unit.

After sleeping like the dead, Gloria returns home. *To sleep like the dead.* Josie insists on accompanying hir, even though Gloria tells hir there's no need.

'I've nothing else to do,' Josie says.

Ze take the rural-link together, travelling in silence. When ze alight, Gloria doesn't need neupath to sense hir daughter bristling with annoyance as ze reaches for the old-fashioned key ze wears around hir neck.

'I like the feel of it,' ze says out loud, slotting the metal into the lock.

Ze leans into the cottage door to feel the weight of hir body against its surface and to experience the reassuring mechanical shift as ze turns the key. Retinarec offers no such reassurance. Josie follows hir inside, hir bodies momentarily crammed next to one another's in the narrow porch. The G-sound that usually fills Gloria's cottage has been silenced and a tide mark runs around the scrubbed walls. Josie tells hir via neupath that ze can get that dealt with.

'I'd prefer it if you would speak out loud when we're here,' Gloria reminds hir daughter. Hir home, hir rules.

Ze remembers 'as long as you're living under my roof' arguments, but ze can't be sure whether ze were rows ze had with hir own parents or with a teenage Josie. Ze checks hir imagometer, but the memory isn't strong enough, it doesn't register. Some things are beyond G-recol.

The next day, ze receives a reminder to visit the artist's studio via G-lore. Ze is tired from hir stay at Josie's, so ze opts for G-real. Neupath info directs hir to an upper floor and ze chooses to take the stairs instead of elevate. Gripping the handrail, ze realises the warm, smooth, surface under hir fingers is planed wood. This part of the G-lore building must be roman-ninety, or more. Ze climbs the stairs, pausing for breath halfway up. The stairwell smells of dust and paint, a mix ze recognises from some long-ago place. The light here is natural, falling in lopsided shadows instead of uniform lo-glo.

At the top of the stairs is a blue door—greasy marks around the handle show where others have been. Gloria pushes it open. The door gives on to a bright room, noisy with the chatter of around twenty people, mostly elders, who are gathered, some standing, some sitting, among a forest of easels. Windows all around the room look out into the tops of trees, the leaves pressing against the glass.

'Welcome,' says a woman, who must be the instructor. She moves towards Gloria and reaches out a hand in the old-fashioned way that Daddy used to greet folk. The woman's hair is dreadlocked and the colour of copper. She wears it gathered on top of her head. Her skin shows recessive sun damage—rare, since the screen-scheme. She reminds Gloria of someone. It's like looking in the mirror, a mirror showing her younger self. You'd think G-recol would have produced such a mirror.

'They have produced one, you're looking at it,' someone says, but she can't see who's talking, and the woman has taken Gloria's other hand and is smiling at Gloria, pulling her into the room. The other participants ignore Gloria. The woman's grasp is warm and firm. She must be the teacher, Gloria thinks again, but no neupath confirmation is forthcoming. She leads Gloria to an empty easel.

'You have this one,' the woman says.

'I'm Gloria,' Gloria tells her.

'That's glorious,' the woman replies, and she laughs lightly as she moves away, weaving around the room pinning fresh white squares of paper on to each easel. The hem of her loose, flowing clothing skims the paint-spattered floor.

'How do I...I'm a beginner,' Gloria says. 'I've not done anything like this before.' But her voice is lost in the noise and clatter of other people taking up their positions around her. All around, folk are arranging pots and brushes, adjusting the angle of their easels. She is surprised to notice a man among them, an old white guy whose scalp is speckled with age spots, as are the backs of his hands.

He reminds Gloria of the one-legged boss she had when she was young. His clothes are crisp and pressed, and he wears a bunch of keys on his belt.

'How do I begin?' Gloria asks out loud, but no one answers, and no one looks at her.

Leaves rustle at the windows and the clamour is soon replaced with a soft scratching and sighing as participants map out their compositions on the paper in front of them.

The instructor comes to her side and whispers, 'What we're creating is a wash.'

The last time Gloria heard someone whisper was a long time ago. It's a habit that has died out. She leans towards the woman who, in her lowered voice, invites her to look out of the leaf-smudged windows and approximate the colour of what she sees. The woman plucks a paintbrush from behind her ear and waggles it in a jar of water so that the glass tinkles. She hands the brush to Gloria.

All Gloria can see is leaves. She can taste the cruciferous green that fills the room. Her eyes are full of it, her body trembles with it. She shivers the paintbrush against emerald paste then transfers it to the paper. The mark she makes fills her with a kind of silvery lightness that seems to expand inside her. As she hovers the paintbrush over the palette, her mind fills with other colours. She is flooded with warm gold. She dabs the brush and makes another mark and then another. Soon the white square is covered with metallic stabs of light, fading to soft shades of apricot and pink, deepening to crimson and ruby red, with patches of mineral green. She peels it off the easel and floats it to the studio floor where it lies damply against others she has produced, without even knowing, their different colours mingling.

When she looks up, the room is empty, apart from the teacher who is washing paintbrushes in an old-fashioned sink. There is no hum from a Haier, only the rush of water and the delicate clatter of brushes on porcelain. The young woman turns from the sink, wiping her hands on her clothes. She approaches Gloria, and Gloria waits for an alert telling her the session is over now, but instead the woman puts her arm around Gloria's shoulder. They stand together, side by side, facing her easel. She has painted the island where Daddy lived, and she has painted the garden she gardened. She rests her head against the teacher's shoulder. She will come again, she thinks, to this peculiar room drenched with its strange, leafy light. The smell of the studio fills her nostrils and she can still feel the wooden handrail under her fingers. Her breathlessness halfway up the stairs was a nice touch. She thinks about asking if this is G-reality, but as Tutz would say, what does it matter? G-loria closes hir eyes. Hir imagometer flickers.

Woman of the Year

YOU RECEIVED an invitation to a formal luncheon celebrating 'Woman of the Year'. You don't know who sent the invite, which is handwritten on ridged, cream card and stands on a bookshelf in your bedroom so you can look at it before you go to sleep and when you wake up. The invitation reminds you that someone thinks highly of you, considers you worth inviting, wants to celebrate you.

You know the building where the event is to be held, but you have never been there. It's the new-old library, a glass building so tall it can be seen from the ring road.

You shower, slip a dress over your head, put on your sandals and are ready. You walk through the park and join the footpath that follows the river out of town. You have allowed plenty of time. You keep one hand on the bag strapped across your body, which contains the precious invitation. There's an odd light in the sky and a strange smell on the breeze, something sweet, maybe? Bright sunlight in a dark sky suggests there could be a storm later. Apart from a small brown bird that flits alongside you, sharing your journey, you see no one else. There are no passers-by, and no one is following you. The bird darts in and out of bushes and hedgerows, sometimes flying ahead, sometimes dropping behind so you can hear the rustle of its wings at your back. The river is flowing fast and where it rushes over the weir, the smell in the air intensifies, fresh, metallic almost, caught in the leaves of the overhanging trees. You watch your feet as you walk.

Soon, the river path widens into flat plains and the library looms against the strange, violet clouds. The wind is up, the breeze of earlier has become tougher, whipping branches and rearranging your hair. The air is warm, though—this must be a desert wind. You cross dry, scrubby grass and quicken your step, feeling your chest tighten as you approach the enormous building. Its previous edifice, made from red Victorian brick, can be seen through the shimmering glass portico, a building inside a building.

You pass in between the cars parked in the car park. Their metal is hot to your touch and leaves a dusty residue on your fingers. An unsmiling security man at the door holds up a hand and asks for your name. You fumble in your handbag for the invitation and when you show him the card with your name on it, he nods, unclasps the black cord that hangs across the library entrance and allows you inside.

It's cooler indoors than outdoors, the foyer is air-conditioned and you wish you had worn a jacket. Someone rushes forward, a tall woman in a black trouser suit.

'Is it you? It must be! We've been waiting for you!'

The material of her suit is stretched taut. She has a broad, heavy body and curly blonde hair. A name sticker on her lapel has 'Carlotta' written on it in neat capital letters. You apologise for being late and she tells you that you aren't late, you're on time. She peels off a blank sticker from a sheet she holds and offers it to you on an outstretched fingertip. You take the sticker and the marker pen she hands you and write your name on the label.

'We're all here now,' Carlotta tells the sullen security guy.

You press your name sticker to your breast.

'Follow me,' Carlotta says. 'They won't serve lunch without everyone and we're all starving!'

She leads you through some double doors into a huge, vaulted room, full of people seated around tables. It's warmer in here. The windows are floor-to-ceiling, and the tables are laid with cutlery and glassware and covered with starched white cloths. Libraries used to be for books, but there are no books in sight. The cathedral-like space is full of tinkling chatter bouncing off the glass surfaces. Everyone seems to know one another. Carlotta shows you to a table where ten or more women are already seated.

'This is us,' she says, and pulls out a chair, gesturing for you to sit.

'Hi,' whispers a woman in the seat next to yours. She holds a sleeping baby in her arms.

Carlotta sits on the other side of you, drawing her chair tightly into the table so that the table edge presses against her body. She rests her hands on the white linen cloth.

'I've never been here before,' you say.

'Nor me,' Carlotta says. 'She used to work here.' She points at a young woman sitting on the other side of the table who has a boyish haircut and wears an odd kind of pinafore. Her name sticker has 'Cassie' written on it.

'I was in archives. It was a long time ago,' Cassie says. 'I work somewhere else now.'

'None of us know who invited us,' Carlotta goes on. 'Do you?'

The other women look at you, expectantly. You tell them you have no idea who invited you here.

'It's a mystery,' says a smartly dressed older woman on the other side of Carlotta—Cecile, according to the label stuck to her navy jacket. She is tiny, with a chic, jaw-length haircut. You can't be sure, but you think her accent might be French.

'Who cares as long as we get a posh meal out of it,' says a younger woman next to her, whose accent is definitely not French, and whose choice of clothing is more casual than everyone else's. She peels her name sticker off her tracksuit top before you can read it, and rolls it into a thin cylinder, then discards it on the table.

Apart from Tracksuit Girl and a girl of around fourteen, or so, sitting further around the table, who wears a school uniform, everyone is dressed formally, as if for a party or a wedding. A scruffy-looking older woman is even wearing a pillbox hat. Her name is scrawled so messily, in a peculiar curling script, it's impossible to read. The schoolgirl keeps her head bowed, concentrating on something under the table—her phone, presumably. There's an empty chair between the young woman in the tracksuit and the next guest, who is quite heavily pregnant.

'This arrived in the post,' you say, digging inside your bag and bringing out your invitation.

Your movement makes the baby on your left stir in its mother's lap. It opens its eyes briefly, but the mother strokes her child's forehead and its eyelids flutter closed once more.

'None of us know who sent them,' says Carlotta.

'We've worked out there are twenty-six tables,' says the schoolgirl, looking up from her device. 'One for each letter of the alphabet.'

'All our names begin with C,' Carlotta says.

'And all ze ladies on that table 'ave names beginning with un B,' says Cecile, the little French lady. 'I know because my daughter is one of them.' She nods her head at the table next to us, where a waiter wearing black gloves and a pristine white jacket is pouring water into glasses.

'Your daughter's here?' Carlotta asks. 'Which one is she?'

Cecile points her out, and you can hear her complaining to Carlotta that her daughter doesn't go by the name her own mother gave her and that, strictly speaking, she should be on a different table.

'Ah, it's nice to have her close by, though, eh?' Carlotta says, smiling.

'Pff!' Cecile says.

'Are we expecting anyone else?' the pregnant woman asks, gesturing to the empty seat between her and Tracksuit Girl.

'I'm pretty certain we're all here,' Carlotta says. Then she whispers in your ear, 'There was meant to be someone else coming, but I heard she died. So sad.'

You hear the pregnant woman ask Tracksuit Girl her name.

'Call me Caz,' she says, her voice loud and brash.

A waiter brings a carafe of water to the table.

'Is there wine?' Cecile asks him, but he doesn't reply, gliding smoothly away and returning moments later with champagne.

'Don't mind if I do,' says Caz, holding out her glass. The solemn-faced waiter moves round to serve her. He holds one hand behind his back while he pours the wine.

'Poncey,' Caz says, grinning.

'Leave the bottle, why don't you?' Cecile suggests, but he takes it away with him.

You watch him join a number of other waiters who stand to attention at the swing doors on the other side of the atrium. They stand with their feet planted wide, like soldiers on guard.

Caz takes a sip of champagne and reaches for her rolled up name sticker, bringing it to her lips like a cigarette. She takes a puff, and blows out imaginary smoke.

'Trying to give up,' she tells her pregnant neighbour.

The pregnant woman smiles. 'Do you want my champagne?' she asks. 'I'm not drinking.' She pushes her glass along the table.

'When are you due?' Carlotta asks, and there is a moment of confusion when Caz thinks she is addressing her.

'Can you tell?' she asks, then realises her mistake. 'Oh, you mean her.'

'Are you expecting, too?' the pregnant woman asks Caz.

'Yeah—not as soon as you, though, by the looks of it.' She pulls off her tracksuit top. 'I'm not even showing yet and I'm ten weeks.' She asks the woman sitting opposite her, 'Don't you want to take your coat off? I'm sweating out.'

The other woman shakes her head and makes no move to unbutton her coat. 'Charlotte' is written on her name sticker in old-fashioned handwriting. She seems nervous, her eyes darting between the guests, not talking to the women on either side of her—'Caro', who has dreadlocks, and the scruffy older woman in the hat.

There's a brief moment of awkwardness as everyone around the table tries not to look at her. Now a woman from another table comes over. She is hippy-looking, her mousey hair is in dreadlocks too, tied back with a printed scarf, her bare arms are tattooed. She bends over to talk to the eldest guest at your table, who sits on the other side of Caro.

'There's a spare place, if you want to sit with us,' Caro tells the hippyish woman, who thanks her and says that would be lovely.

'Would you like that, Clem?' the hippy woman asks her elderly friend, enunciating her words carefully.

The old woman smiles at her with a mild expression. She looks quite fragile and seems to shiver. Caro gets Caz to pass the spare plate and cutlery across the table, while the hippy woman drags the empty chair around, her bangles clattering against the furniture. Once she's settled, you hear her compliment Caro on the silk blouse she is wearing, which is crinkled and un-ironed and printed all over with sunflowers. She tells Caro how she and the frail old lady know each other. 'We met in the middle of the night, didn't we, Clem?' she says, but you don't hear the rest of the story because a man in neatly tailored trousers and a white shirt mounts a podium and announces that lunch is served. At his words, the waiters spring into action, disappearing through the swing doors.

'Hey, that's cool,' Caz says, tilting her head back and swivelling around in her chair to view the glass ceiling, the full three-hundred-and-sixty-degree skyscape, her ponytail dangling. The dark clouds from earlier have been replaced by delicate blue skies. The threatening storm seems to have passed. The women are laughing and chatting and sunlight pours into the room, lighting up the silver cutlery and sparkling glasses. Waiters reappear, carrying silver dishes piled with vegetables.

The baby next to you has woken up. He has been lying in his mother's lap, also gazing up at the ceiling, but now he begins to kick his little legs and his mother sits him upright.

The slovenly older woman gives his foot a little tug and coos at him. The baby stares at her and then takes in all the faces around the table. Evidently, he decides he doesn't like what he sees, and he lets out a high-pitched wail. The scruffy-looking woman recoils slightly, shifting her chair away from him.

'Typical—as soon as the food arrives,' Caro says. 'Mine were the same.' As waiters vanish behind the swing doors and return carrying unfeasible numbers of plates balanced along each arm, Caro asks the baby's mother if she would like her to hold the baby so she can eat.

'I'll feed him first,' the mother says. She unclasps her bra and attaches him to her breast, and you see the scruffy old lady avert her eyes.

A plate of food is placed in front of you, but you don't recognise any of the items. There is a smallish ball of what could be rice, except that it has no individual grains. Could it be porridge, perhaps? It's soft and grey. Next to it is a curved object, the size and shape of a banana, toasted and golden, and next to that are some berries and a small puddle of sauce.

'Fish,' Cecile declares, prodding the banana-shaped item with her fork, and this seems likely—when she turns it over it has beautiful markings on its underside.

'I'll just have the vegetables,' says Charlotte, the woman who won't take off her coat. She is quite odd looking, with smooth skin and youthful features, but there's something ancient about her manner, which makes her seem old, or like an Amish person, or a Victorian. She reaches for the dish in the centre of the table, but our waiter intercepts her, scooping up the dish and serving her a portion of vegetables as if she is an invalid, incapable of helping herself. Charlotte sits back obediently in her chair and the waiter works his way around each of us, spooning broccoli, green beans and thinly sliced carrots on to our plates. As soon as he has gone, Charlotte takes a green bean off her plate and you notice her surreptitiously drop it next to her chair.

'Tastes like ackee,' someone says.

It's true, the grey pulpy mixture does taste a bit like ackee, or pureed artichokes, maybe, but no one seems certain what it is. We all take small mouthfuls. Conversation is mainly about the mystery of how we all came to be invited here. As we speculate on why each of our credentials might earn us a 'Woman of the Year' nomination, people ask each other what they do for a living. You overhear the hippy woman talking about her work as a zoologist. When someone asks what her area of research is, she explains she studies copulatory wounding in flies.

'Copulatory wounding?'

'Yes, the male fly's penis gets pinched between the—'

'Wait, you're telling me flies have dicks?' laughs Caz.

'Of course,' the zoologist replies.

A woman on a neighbouring table overhears our conversation and asks what on earth we're talking about.

'Flies' cocks!' yells Caz.

Cecile tuts loudly and scolds her for being vulgar.

'But it's true,' Caz exclaims, 'ask her!'

'I spend most of my working day examining flies' vaginas under a microscope,' the zoologist admits.

There's a stunned, momentary silence.

'Their teeny tiny vaginas,' Charlotte whispers, and the zoologist's elderly friend gives a small sigh.

'I'm seeing someone who knows all about clams,' says Charlie, the woman who's sitting opposite you. Her name sticker is written in chubby, round handwriting, with the dot of the 'i' made into a flower.

You watch as she gets into conversation with the guests sitting either side of her. The quiet woman on her left tries to include the schoolgirl in their chat, but although the girl is polite, she returns her attention as soon as she can to whatever it is that's on her lap. As she talks, Charlie dreamily rubs the fabric of her dress between her fingers. It has floaty sleeves made of chiffony material. Meanwhile, every now and then, the schoolgirl glances up, then quickly down again, and you wonder if it might not be a phone she is concentrating on, after all, but a drawing pad, perhaps. Maybe she's sketching us.

All of a sudden, the scruffy old lady gives a yelp. 'She's got a frog!' she squawks, lifting the tablecloth and pushing her chair away from the table.

Charlotte shushes her and asks her to be quiet.

'Show 'em!' the scruffy lady says.

'I'm not sure people will be keen...while they're eating...'

But everyone wants to see the frog. Charlotte hesitates, then bends down to reach under the table, re-emerging to place a frog next to her plate. The frog wears a tiny, frilly lace cap and an expression as solemn as one of the waiters.

'It's big for a frog,' observes the hippy zoologist.

'Are you sure it's not a toad?' asks Caro.

'Hush!' Charlotte says, adjusting the frog's bonnet and placing her hands where its ears might be. 'Don't let him hear you say that.'

The frog hops to the middle of the table. It's tethered on a slender leather leash, which Charlotte wears looped around her wrist.

'Look, darling,' the mother tells her baby, 'Froggy!'

The first course is over. Caro takes the baby so his mother can eat her meal, and others pick up their interrupted conversations. You can hear Cecile discussing the pregnant woman's situation.

'So who is ze father then, if your partner is a woman?' she asks.

'We went for a donor, in the end,' comes the answer.

'Saves a whole bunch of trouble,' Caz says, fiddling with her rolled up name sticker once more, taking a puff then tapping imaginary ash.

'Oh, we'll have trouble of our own, I'm sure,' the pregnant woman says.

Caz lets out a harsh laugh. 'True dat!'

'Oui, c'est vrai,' Cecile says, pursing her lips and nodding sagely.

The baby isn't happy, straining towards his mother and screwing up his face.

'Oh, come on, now,' Caro murmurs. 'Let Mummy have her special lunch.'

The baby stretches his arms out, beseeching. His mother lays down her knife and fork, ready to take him back, when the scruffy woman produces a pom-pom keyring and dangles it in front of his face.

'He likes that,' says Charlie, who has moved around the table and is squatting next to Caro, trying to help soothe him.

'My Chinese friend gave it to me,' the scruffy woman tells her.

Charlotte gives up her chair to Charlie, lifting the frog's lead over the heads of the other diners as she swaps places.

You're still hungry, and so are others. The quiet woman who tried to talk to the schoolgirl is looking forward to dessert, and as she says as much, pudding arrives. Everyone is relieved it's chocolate. 'My favourite,' says the quiet woman, who you've noticed speaks with a Welsh accent. Charlotte asks her how she keeps her figure. 'I don't really think about it,' she says.

'But you must!' Cecile declares.

The quiet woman flushes slightly and tells us she plays netball. 'But just for fun,' she says.

Overhead, the sky is growing dark again. A canopy of lurid mauve cloud hangs over the building, looking as if it might split at any moment. The catering manager in the sharp trousers flicks a switch, and thousands of tiny lights come on. A kind of twilight descends. There is a lull in conversation while we scrape our bowls and smack our lips. Heavy spots of rain begin to pock the windows as the guest speaker for the afternoon is announced. The speaker is the daughter of a captain of industry none of us have heard of.

'Can you hear me alright?' the man's daughter asks, as a loud clap of thunder sounds and a sharp, torrential downpour spatters against the glass. 'That's the trouble with these so-called intelligent buildings,' she says. 'No one can hear you when you're inside them!'

But as she speaks a microphone on a slim silver stand rises out of the podium.

'Oh!' she says. 'I do beg your pardon.'

She looks around to see who might be guiding the instrument, but there is no one. The microphone adjusts itself to her height and angles itself towards her mouth. She embarks on a speech about her father's life, sharing adventure stories and humorous anecdotes, as well as tales of his fiscal daring. The frail old lady is nodding off in her hippy friend's tattooed arms, her body moving gently up and down as she snores. It's not clear whether it's her breath causing the rocking motion, or her friend's cradling. You can hear a sound of water trickling, a higher note than the rain outside. It's close by and quite loud. The waiters and their manager have noticed it too, and begin feeling along walls, trying to locate pipes that have burst, maybe. We begin to talk among ourselves, with Connie, the scruffy old woman, regaling us with tales of her modelling days. Caz and the schoolgirl are mucking about with the pet frog, and Charlie entertains the baby by playing peekaboo, covering her face with a napkin and whipping it off again. You think we're all being a bit bad mannered, and it's true, the guest speaker has prepared her speech and we've been served a fancy meal, the least we can do is listen. But none of us are interested in the Captain of Industry, even if he is the speaker's father.

People get up and creep around the table, discreetly swapping places so we can hear one another above the storm and the sound of rushing water without talking loudly enough to disturb the speaker. Women on other tables are doing the same and some are on their phones, covering their mouths with their hands while they take business calls or ring home to check on their kids. Charlie is bouncing the baby on her lap now, quietly singing 'This is the Way the Gentlemen Ride', while you get into a whispered conversation with Cecile, who asks if you plan on having children.

'Make sure you are prrrrepared for your 'ole life to change,' she says, rolling her Rs theatrically.

At last, the speaker comes to the end of her father's life story, and it's only now we notice the catering staff seem to be in a state of panic, hurrying in and out of the kitchen. The manager has put on a hi-vis tabard over his clothes and he stands at the back of the room, eyes wide, drawing a hand back and forth across this throat, signalling to the speaker that she should wind up her speech.

'And so, to conclude, you are all women of the year,' the speaker says, trying to maintain her poise.

'We coulda told you that!' Caz yells, but the speaker ignores her, hastily pulling out a trophy and raising her voice above the sound of rushing water to tell us how great we are.

The trophy is made from glass and has a clown's face on it, etched in gold. As the speaker holds it aloft, one of the waiters shouts, 'Flood!' Chairs scrape back and we run to the windows to look outside.

Water is rising—not dirty water coming from the river, but clear water, inching up the glass windows so the place is like a fish tank in reverse—we are the fishes, colourful and exotic in our outfits. We stand up from our tables and move to the edges of the room, going to the windows to look out, our hands pressed against the glass.

'Where's it coming from?' the schoolgirl asks.

'From all around,' you tell her, because that's how it seems to you.

You spot the notebook she's holding, its pages hanging open, full of busy handwriting. Rain batters the skylights and the waiters cower, as if they are afraid the ceiling might fall in. People get on their phones, and word quickly goes round that roads are cut off and we are unreachable. The catering manager scurries through the banqueting room in his fluorescence, bashing in and out of the swing doors. Water is rising quickly—it's waist level already, and not clear any more, but brownish and foaming. Us women turn to each other, wondering if it would be better to leave or whether it's safer to stay where we are.

'I'm quite a strong swimmer,' the mother of the young baby says. 'But what about him?' She looks over to where Charlie and the scruffy older woman are playing with her child.

Cassie suggests we take the lift to one of the higher floors.

'I thought you're not supposed to use a lift in an emergency?' the mother says.

'That's when it's a fire,' Cassie tells her, and she looks around at all of us. 'Who's coming?'

No one moves. Outside, parked cars nudge one another like restless horses, their noses touching when they weren't before. A red Volvo at the far end of the car park has swivelled forty-five degrees and its back end lifts slightly before the water carries it jostling past the windows.

'My car!' the catering guy yells, running up and down with his hands in his hair.

We watch the vehicle get carried downstream, followed by other objects—a shoe, an armchair, a bike, a shopping trolley, a child's high chair, a hula hoop. We are entranced, somehow, by the storm and by the strange light. The mother takes her baby from Charlie and holds him close. The building is groaning now, and with a loud crack, a jagged line zigzags its way from the top of one of the windows to the bottom. Women step away just in time as the great wall of glass crashes inwards, smashing and splintering and shattering over the tables. Cold air whips through the building and waiters scream as water rushes in. We're knee-deep in seconds. Cassie's shouting at us to follow her up to the roof, but some of us want to get out of the building. Someone spots the catering manager wading out in his hi-vis tabard towards his car. People cry out to try and stop him, but he can't hear us. The rushing water tugs at his clothes, knocks him off his feet. The current pulls him along and he has to hold on to a lamppost to anchor himself. His shirt clings to his arms and we watch in horror as the water drags off his trousers and then his underwear. His penis is ruddy against his pale legs. We watch as the security man throws him the black rope that was cordoning off the entrance to the building, but it's not long enough and the water carries it away. The catering guy climbs the lamppost and he's clinging there, calling out to security above the rush of the filthy water. He hunches there like an albino monkey, crying for his mother, crying out for someone to rescue him. And there is no one here but us.

Acknowledgements

Thank you, Candida Lacey, for your ongoing support and vision, and thank you, Vicki Heath Silk for mad editing skills. Grateful thanks to the Royal Literary Fund Fellowship scheme, which provided financial security while I was compiling these stories. Warm thanks to Chetna Maroo, Claire Keegan, Bethan Roberts and Bosie Vincent, who were kind enough to read and comment on work in progress. Thanks to my sister, Bek, for the beautiful cover painting, and thank you to my dear friend Ros, who knows me for the clown I am. Thanks and love, always, to Alvy and Ned, who appreciated my clowning when they were little and who continue to tolerate it.

Original Sources

'She-Clown' was shortlisted for the Manchester Writing Competition 2017, and the Words & Women competition 2017.

'The Poison Frog' was broadcast on BBC Radio 4 in July 2016, produced by Sweet Talk Productions.

MORE SHORT FICTION
FROM MYRIAD

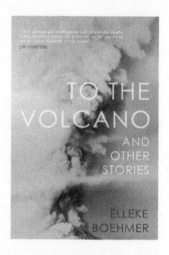

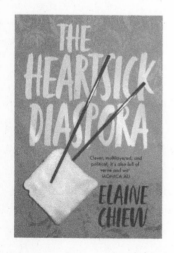

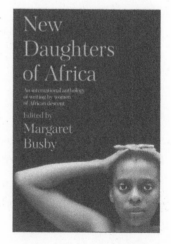

MORE FICTION FROM MYRIAD

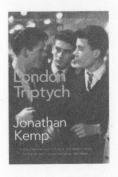

MORE FICTION FROM MYRIAD

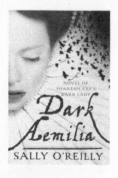

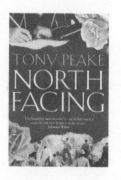

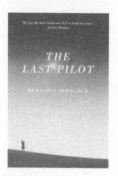

Sign up to our mailing list at
www.myriadeditions.com
Follow us on Facebook and Twitter

About the author

HANNAH VINCENT is a novelist and playwright. She has a PhD in Creative and Critical Writing from the University of Sussex and is the author of two novels, *Alarm Girl* and *The Weaning*.